THROUGH THE BRIAR DOOR

MATCH TENBRINK

Pages Promotions, LLC
1590 Northwoods Drive
Alger, MI 48619
www.PagesPromotions.com

© 2026 Match TenBrink aka Benjamin McCarthy
Edited by Diana Kathryn Penn

Benjamin McCarthy has asserted his right under the Copyright Act to be identified as the Author of this work, writing under the pseudonym Match TenBrink..

Paperback ISBN: 978-1628283884
E-Book ISBN: 978-1628283433
Library of Congress Control Number: On File

DEDICATION:

This collection is dedicated to my love, the one and only

Rose TenBrink.

You showed me what it means to believe in myself again, pushing me to chase my dreams. It was because you believed in me from the very beginning....

where all good stories must start.

For my children, may you forever chase your dreams.

ACKNOWLEDGEMENTS

Rose TenBrink

J.A. Bullen

Haley Hawes

TABLE OF CONTENTS

FOREWORD

Reading Through the Briar Door immediately invokes a time in my life when I sat in my pajamas, watching as *The Crypt Keeper* came on screen to deliver my latest bedtime story. As I write this foreword, I feel a certain obligation to slip into my robe and slippers and kick up my feet in front of the fireplace as I deliver my best Vincent Price impersonation.

If you've found yourself here because, like me, you are ever curious about the creative process, then you are in for a treat. While I have a personal favorite, I carry a fondness for each of these stories. Be it their unconventional twists, the thrill of the unknown as the protagonist risks it all, or even the buildup to what feels like part one of another, larger story, there is a wealth of suspense in the coming pages.

However, I encourage everyone to take the time to read through the pages beyond my ramblings here. Enrich yourself in the words, lessons, and chills. Grow and be inspired by the various tales. I hope each of you who finds this collection takes something from it.

- J.A. Bullen – Author of sensorial fantasies epic, dark, and urban.

- www.meetthebullens.com
- Facebook - @jabulle
- Twitter - @JA_Bullen

THROUGH THE BRIAR DOOR

Dry leaves crunch under the weight of every step,
A dense atmosphere through this dark forest begins to ebb,
Fear grows rampant inside your mind,
As darkness falls, you look for somewhere to hide.

What is this? You suddenly ask yourself,
It appears to be a briar patch. Nothing else,
Your eyes deceive you as you begin to see more,
For it appears there exists a very small door.

Should you continue or turn never to come back,
What horrors or nightmares hide, waiting to attack?
Yet, in some way, you are drawn to just that,
Despite the lesson foreboding the cat.

A lesson in which curiosity killed forevermore,
Suddenly you realize your life is a bore,
The thorns cut deep as you embrace the fear in store,
Now steel your nerves as you enter…

Through the Briar Door

THE SUNFLOWER FESTIVAL

Each yellow line that she passed began to annoy her. *Overisel*, where the hell was that, anyway? A two-cow town. If you blinked, you missed it. Is this what she had come to? She went from breaking shock and awe stories to reporting on fluff stories.

Breaking news: the otter at the local zoo had babies; how the local cookie shop created a new whipped topping and Elma Potternose turned 102 years old.

"Jesus, Susan," she muttered over the fuzzy radio, desperately holding onto the signal of the country station back home.

The Annual Sunflower Festival was coming up in Overisel. They won Greatest Flower Town in the quad county area each year. They held onto this title for over a decade, which they apparently held with pride. She passed a billboard with the proclamation in six-foot-high letters accompanied by their bright yellow floral mascot.

Truth be told, they were supposed to have breathtaking fields absolutely filled to the brim with Sunflowers for miles. However, she wasn't here to report on the annual sunflower fields. Oh no, she was here to regain her status as the hard-nosed reporter who shattered lies, uncovered the most scandalous stories, and revealed them to the world.

✳✳✳✳

A woman sat at Susan's desk at the Gazette. Susan thought they could be close in age, but the grays highlighting the dark brown hair pulled into a very tight ponytail on her head betrayed this youthful appearance. As she moved with hesitation toward her desk, she noticed the woman sitting nervously, her hands clasped between her legs in her tight-fitting skirt. Her posture in the dark grey suit coat draped neatly around her shoulders, accentuating the shoulder pads, making them point upwards like a character from a foreign cartoon.

"Miss Susan Renault?" No hand stretched out for a handshake. In fact, there was no movement at all.

"Depends on who's asking," Susan coughed a fake chuckle. She really meant this, though. She had made quite a few enemies in her past line of work. *You don't make great omelets without breaking a few yokes.* This became her catch phrase when speaking to her critics.

"I have a story I'd like you to investigate. I understand you aren't afraid to do whatever it takes to bring the truth to life." Then, she leaned in. "I just ask that… I stay anonymous."

This happened to her a few times since starting with the Gazette. However, these people didn't get the memo. She didn't, no, she *couldn't* do stories like that anymore. Due to her biggest flop, she lost everything, and the only place willing to take her told her she could only do soft stories… Heartwarming local news that helped put smiles on simple people's faces. After all, she was no longer in the big city. Like Sisyphus, she had pushed the boulder to the top of the hill only to have it roll all the way back down. The only difference was that she couldn't get out of the way of that rolling boulder.

"I'm sorry, Miss Anonymous," she finally sat down, feeling calmer that it wasn't one of her… many critics. "No one told you? I don't do these stories anymore."

"That's too bad. It's okay. I get it. No one cares about the dead after they are dead, anyway." The lady began to gather her belongings. She carried a large professional leather bag aged with two thick leather handles in the center on each side.

Susan leaned back. *Don't, Susan, don't take the bait.* A few seconds passed before she couldn't take it anymore. Her old chair let out a massive *creak* as she lunged forward.

"Wait, please sit." She paused for a moment, to make sure no one else was listening in the newsroom. "What did you mean by that?"

Miss Anonymous began to explain the juiciest story that had fallen into Susan's lap since her days with the big boys. Apparently, a family practice funeral service existed in the town of Overisel. They were dead-center in four counties, and they were the only funeral service in this rural area. That wasn't a story. It got juicy because it's also the home of the Sunflower Festival.

Miss Anonymous recently started a job as a postmortem make-up artist. The first outside hire this funeral home had ever considered. Apparently, one night, she forgot her purse in the back room. While going to retrieve it, she discovered something so dark it could only have come from a horror movie.

"You see, I had always thought that offering only one style of coffin was a clever way to cut costs and save money, but I was wrong…" She trailed off, and Susan watched her eyes lower to the ground. "So very wrong."

Susan handed a box of Kleenex to her apathetically. It was hard to tell if this lady was going to cry or spew chunks all over the floor before her.

"What they actually do is dump the bodies and swap the coffin out for a more crudely built one. One that is good enough to pass scrutiny when lowered into the ground. I just came back to grab my purse," her hand clenched on the purse in her lap, and she dropped the tissue from her face to join it as she brought her eyes up to meet Susan's gaze. "I just couldn't help it… I gasped…"

"I understand that must've been a pretty awful thing to discover," Susan replaced the box back to her spot on the desk.

"No, you don't understand," she then slammed down her hand and it hit her thigh. "It's not just that they dump the bodies. It's what they do after that."

For Susan, watching that reaction was like waiting for the server to bring out your freshly cooked lobster tail at a restaurant. It's no surprise a visceral reaction like that would hook her. Susan leaned closer, looked both ways to ensure she wasn't gathering unwanted attention, and responded.

"What did you see?"

"They were putting the bodies…" she paused and leaned in herself, "through a meat grinder."

"What?" Susan spewed back in disbelief.

"Then they use it as compost for the Sunflower fields."

The silence lasted only a few seconds, but long enough to feel like minutes.

Miss Anonymous sat straight in her chair. She rubbed her thigh as she finally noticed the pain caused by her own fist. She took a second to smooth out her clothes.

"That's when they gave me a *choice*," she used her fingers in air quotations as she said the last word. "Join in with them, sign an NDA, and start helping. Or…"

"Become compost," Susan finished her sentence.

"My dear, no. That I'd be fired and my name tarnished. I'd have to move miles away and start a new life."

"Oh, okay. That's good."

"Anyway, I tried to play along, but my conscience wouldn't let me anymore. That's when I thought of you." She looked at Susan, pleading, awaiting a reply.

"I'll have to think it over."

"Please do consider it. It's a good time to visit. The sunflowers will be in full bloom you see."

****

"They sure are gorgeous," thought Susan as she scanned through radio stations to find signals, surrounded by the endless fields of sunflowers. They went on for miles. A sickening thought occurred to her, *so human bodies are great fertilizer*. She remembered her younger days as her mom struggled to grow flowers in their micro garden. She recalled her mom's voice complaining that she wished she knew the secret behind having a green thumb.

Finally, a few buildings started to emerge. It was a small downtown area with one street filled with brick buildings for approximately a city block. There was a four-way stop in the center of town, and something inside screamed at Susan. This was the most exciting thing the town would ever see.

That's when she saw it: *Four Corner's Funeral Home*. It wasn't tremdously distinguished from the other buildings in the downtown area. There wasn't anything striking or different. Her neck craned over the dash, trying to study the building. A sign outside read *Remembering Thomas Van Olmstead*. It was written in chalk on a blackboard pylon outside the front door. This, of course, was her cover. An estranged niece who missed her dear Uncle Thomas.

Taking in the building, she was a little disappointed. She wasn't sure exactly what she expected. *Maybe something like Poe would have dreamed up. A gothic gray building adorned with snarling gargoyles and grotesque architectural wonders identifying to all outside that this was a place of grim death.*

Parking was about what one might expect. It was farther away, making her walk a block or so to the building.

The parlor was empty, and there was a faint smell of embalming fluid mixed with floral potpourri as Susan entered. She noticed the caskets and took note that her source was right. They all looked the same. A laden oak door was not stained but made to preserve a natural pine wooden color. There were absolutely no other options.

"Good afta'nun," it took Susan a minute to understand what the older man said as he approached. She glanced at her watch, just past three o'clock. The man was properly dressed in a black suit, white shirt, and black tie. She was certain that all funeral homes required this uniform. It struck her as similar to a Mormon knocking at your door. Except this man didn't have 'good news.'

"Good afternoon," Susan stopped studying the caskets and looked up.

"How may I help you, Missy?" the silver hair bounced as he nodded kindly.

"I'm here for um…" Panic set in. *What was the dead man's name?* "My uncle's funeral."

"Your Uncle? Thomas Van Olmstead?"

"Yes, my Uncle Tom!" She smiled, then quickly allowed it to fade into a frown. She was supposed to be sad.

"I'm sorry; did your family not inform you? The funeral isn't until tomorrow." A smile crossed his face. It was sympathetic but ultimately fake. The sincerity escaped him.

"Oh, my goodness. I must be a day early! I am from out of town," Susan feigned aloofness.

"That happens sometimes," a woman's voice emerged from the back room as she walked into the parlor. It was that same brown hair salted with grays but pulled into a tight ponytail. She acted cool and casual as if she had never seen Susan before.

"Silly me, I must've mistaken the days. I could have sworn I was told the funeral was today."

"It's okay, Miss…" the man inflected.

"Susan," she paused, "Dogherty." Doubtful that they recognized her name in this forgotten Podunk place. Still, she had learned in recent years to be a bit more careful. *Don't want to have to be met at your car again with someone screaming, 'you ruined my life.'* This was her strategy. She created the alias last night.

"Nice to meet you, Miss Dogherty," the kindly old man threw out his hand for a handshake. "I am Johnny DeHaan. I am the caretaker of this quaint little funeral home. Our goal is to make a nice personal experience to remember your uncle."

The woman stepped up, "I am Ashleigh Rutfield, the makeup artist here at the home. We do hope you enjoy your visit. It is a beautiful time to be in Overisel, despite the sad occasion. Did you happen to see the Sunflowers?"

Susan nodded and wondered if Ashleigh could be any more obvious. "I did. They are quite breathtaking. Is it possible to have a tour? It would mean a lot to me to see where the service will take place." Susan thought about how damn good she was at this; the lying.

Johnny obliged her. He was very professional. If this Ashleigh was right, then Johnny did a damn good job of being as cordial as can be. Nothing seemed to be out of place. The only thing that checked out so far was the coffin selection.

It makes sense. If what Ashleigh claimed was truly happening, they wouldn't do it out in the open while people came in to say goodbye to their loved ones.

The tour included the history of the funeral home, the fact that it had been in the family for four generations, and how Overisel started as a Dutch settlement.

"The conservative dress and manner of speaking in this area are a direct result of our Dutch heritage. We are the only funeral home in all four counties." Johnny was quite proud. "Also, the sunflowers that surround this beautiful town isn't just for the appearance. You see Overisel, in fact, relies on this crop for the seed, oil, and other byproducts that we derive from the sunflowers. Truly, if it weren't for the sunflowers our little town would be hurting significantly."

Johnny was interrupted when they reached the reception area, which was presented elegantly for her *Uncle Tom's* wake the next day. A man walked in wearing a white apron covered in red, some splotches darker than others. He was a younger man, covered head to toe in a mask, elbow-length gloves, and blood spotches on his shirt and pants.

"Todd," a flash of anger awoke in Johnny's eyes. "Please excuse my nephew's uncharacteristic entrance. I must go." Quite loudly, he called, "Ashleigh!"

"Yes," she hurried into the room as Johnny ushered Todd away.

"Please complete the tour with Susan."

"Will do," she smiled.

Susan thought this was strange. *Why would anyone in a funeral home come out looking like they were just working in the back of a butcher's counter?* A wave of relief hit her. This was the little interruption she needed; a small nugget of an abnormality. The thought that she was wasting her time vanished from her mind.

Ashleigh waited for them to leave and pretended to continue until they were out of sight.

"I'm so glad you came out," she put a hand on Susan's shoulder. "I don't know how long I can continue working in secret, knowing all this."

"Quiet," Susan listened to make sure they were alone. "Okay, I do think there is something weird going on here. However, a bloody guy walking out of the back room isn't enough to write a piece. I need something more, and I need photos."

Ashleigh walked closer to the casket stand. The pall was draped along the back, ready to be pulled onto the casket when put into place. Glancing back and forth, her head on a pendulum, she urged Susan closer.

"That's the back door." Ashleigh pointed toward the back door. It was camouflaged behind the black drapes. "Tonight, when I go home, I'll leave this door unlocked. Come back at seven o'clock, and you can take all the pictures you want."

Then, there was a jarring transition. Susan was still close to Ashleigh when she started her tour speech again, the increase in volume piercing her ear.

"That is the tour of our beautiful accommodations. You see, here at the Four Corners, we truly care about your loved ones and we want to make sure we have a special place for remembrance. Now Miss Susan, I believe," then she gave Susan a wink and sly smile; "Do you have a favorite flower? I hope it's Sunflowers!"

As Ashleigh finished saying this, she used arm gestures to guide her toward the exit. Her jovial customer service voice was grating to Susan.

"Sure thing." Susan thanked her and offered her hand to Ashleigh.

"No, please. Let us thank you from the bottom of our hearts and our deepest condolences about your Uncle." It was so fake. Then, with a smile and a whisp of cool summer air, she opened the front door. "I will surely see you tomorrow."

****

Later that afternoon, Susan lay in her bed at the local motel. It was a modest set of rooms located on the second floor of a local restaurant. Basic cable in a time when most bed and breakfasts had several subscription services seemed archaic to her. Judging by the TV's appearance, she'd be surprised if this place even had WIFI. Men and women in low resolution argued back and forth, but Susan heard nothing. The sound was muted while she scribbled in her notebook.

Suddenly, there was a tin-sounding pitter-patter on the metal roof. Outside the window, the clear sky had become gray overcast as the rain beat down onto the window in waves. *It appears that tonight, I'll be getting wet.* Concerned, she glanced over at her SLR camera sitting on her bedside table. It was an expensive camera. She'd need to find a way to keep it dry. *I bet the town is celebrating tonight, as the rain waters their precious Sunflowers, never realizing they've been fed by the bodies of their loved ones long since passed.*

A memory flashed in her brain about the fateful evening of the corporate espionage case she cracked a few years ago.

****

It was storming outside when her editor called her.

"Susan," she could hear the rain in the background.

"Yes."

"It's about the last story you did. You verified your sources, correct?"

"Oh, he confirmed. I have my ways." She cracked a smile her editor couldn't see.

"I don't give a shit about your ways. I don't even want to know." His voice was stern with a hint of trouble behind it. "They're suing us, Susan. For defamation."

The next few months were straight out of a nightmare. Susan was a tough girl, but her unconventional methods were put on display, and she became known as the 'homewrecking reporter who was wrong.' It turned out the man feeding her information got one thing incorrect. The account that had funded the espionage was off by two numbers and turned out to be the employee scholarship fund. It didn't matter that the crime truly occurred. The newspaper was sued, Susan lost her job, and so much more.

All she had was her reputation, and after that fiasco, it had been dragged through the streets and ended in the garbage.

****

She wore a dark green poncho to protect herself, the notebook, and most importantly, the camera from the cascading rain. Her hood created an amphitheater of raindrops in her ears. It was past seven o'clock, and that was by design. The days were long in early summer, but the overcast gave her cover as she tried to venture down the back alley. The alleyway connected both sides of the buildings, making up their downtown, albeit as small as it was. She passed trash dumpsters outside local restaurants and floral shops. Unexpectedly, the tantalizing aroma reminded her that she never ate dinner.

Counting the buildings, she came upon what she figured would be the funeral home's back door. It was not labeled, of course. There was a protruded extension after the man-door with a gray roll-up garage-style door. It seemed a bit odd for a funeral home. Pulling out her camera, she took a few shots. *Don't know where it might go, but I'd rather have it than not. Could be important.*

With a quick check of the area, she made sure no one was looking and went for the handle. This was the real test. Did her source come through?

Click.

"Yes," she proclaimed quietly as she slowly opened the door. Peeking her head in, she made sure she couldn't see anyone. It was dark; not even a single light was on.

Slowly, she entered and allowed the door to shut behind her. She stood silently for several long seconds before deciding to move again, just to ensure she truly was alone. Then, out of her poncho pocket, she extracted a small flashlight. It was big enough to light her way but small enough not to be overtly noticeable.

God, how I've missed this!

A rush came over her whole body; her hair stood on end, and she tingled with excitement. She was a bit turned on, as well. She felt like a female version of James Bond. Dumb stories about how many puppies the local Puppy Boutique just received were not why she paid out the ass for university tuition. This was it. All those good vibes came rushing in, and she felt electric.

"Alright," she whispered to herself confidently. "Where am I?" She noticed as she lit her torch that she was again in the visitation room. Her light went toward the direction that guy came out all bloody. It was the one area she didn't get to see on the tour. "What juicy, diabolical wonders lay behind that door?" She was riding her high.

She pressed the cold metal door with her hand and slid it open. "Odd, a pocket door; not what I expected." After stepping inside, she stopped and listened carefully before closing the door and flipped the switch. Her torch went back into her pocket, and she pulled out her camera.

"Alright, Susan, do your thing!"

So far, everything looked normal. No surprises. It wasn't going to be so apparent. She switched from James Bond to Kolchak as she investigated the abnormal. "What doesn't seem to fit in?" she mumbled.

In the right corner opposite the door were three caskets. She walked to them after taking several pictures of the layout. One by one, she opened them, curious as to what she would find. The first two were empty. The third held an elderly man with white hair and sunken eyes and cheeks. This man hadn't been alive for a while.

"Uncle Tom, of course. I'm so sorry we had to meet this way." She snapped a picture. "Hope you're excited to become fertilizer." Her voice was almost at a normal tone now. She was comfortable with the fact that she was alone.

Nothing screamed *evidence* yet. What she saw so far looked exactly like everything she had researched about funeral homes. There were several stainless steel tables. It resembled an operating room. There was nothing that showed any butcher-like behavior. She was thorough, though. Susan had enough to be suspicious and prayed this wasn't a bust. Just who she prayed to was not clear, but she wished there would be something story-worthy to find. She had a hunch, and usually, she had good hunches.

Strange tools, weird saws, and strange wrenches sat beside the stainless table. Everything was clean and shiny. There was not a spot of blood on any of the tools. Saw teeth spoke to her, screaming how easily it would be to cut through the bone. Still, there was no evidence of it. Everything was spotless, almost too clean.

In fact, everything in this room seemed to be right where it was supposed to be. Clean, sanitized, and organized better than a dentist's office during Halloween. No bone fragments. No blood stains. No guts or skin pieces. Part of her wished that she'd stumbled upon Dahmer's basement and expected to see lamp shades made of skin or, at the very least, a potted plant of sunflowers with fingers reaching out of the potting soil, reaching to the sky for saving.

"It seems that this is a bust." Everything Susan had hoped for was dashed before her eyes. Ashleigh, it appeared, was full of gruff, and now Susan felt embarrassed. "What the hell am I doing here?"

Grabbing her camera in frustration and shoving it into her poncho, she began to walk toward the door. Then, a metallic shine caught her eye. It was hidden rather well underneath the counter to her left. Deciding she'd rather at least be thorough rather than leaving frustrated, she checked it out.

Whatever it was, it was on wheels, so she could easily pull it out. It was as tall as her waist. It was rather large and clumsy, but she managed to pull it out of its space. It was marked with stainless parts and an overall white plastic casing. There was a large pipe on the top. Like a port hole. On the front side was a smaller pipe angled down like a spout on a bathtub, but much larger. There was a lever with a latching mechanism on the top of the port hole.

Squeak went the latch as she pulled it back. The red vinyl covering on the handle was surprisingly warm to the touch. A large cylindrical shape slid out as she pulled it back. She bent over and peered inside. Her heart stopped, and she backed away, nearly crashing into the table behind her.

This is an oversized meat grinder.

Slowly, her hand reached into her pocket for her camera. Her heartbeat raced, and her pulse thumped inside her head. *This is the key. What would a funeral home be doing with an industrial-sized meat grinder?* Snapping a few pictures, she began to ponder to herself. She wanted to run out and get this to press quickly, but it wasn't enough. *I need more.*

It couldn't happen again. She had to make sure she wouldn't be called out again. That would surely put an end to her career. Technically, she was trespassing. But a*t least this time, I didn't have to sleep with someone to get the proof.* She promised herself she wouldn't go to those lengths again. Still, inside, she knew she'd do anything to get the story, including opening up a potential human meat grinder for proof.

There were buckles on the front so that it could be opened up for cleaning. She released the clasps. It was filled with different interlocking gears. They were surprisingly large and disappointingly clean. It looked like a collection of grinding gears stacked upon one another, all feeding into the spout. She easily imagined this machine was strong enough to crush bone.

Still, it was spotless. Except for the very bottom. There still was some blood there. She snapped a few pictures and then noticed something farther back. She reached in, past all the femur-crushing gears, and felt something hard. She pulled on it and then immediately dropped it with a loud gasp.

It's a tooth!

Suddenly, the bell over the door gave a jingle, and then the door slammed shut.

"Oh shit," she muttered under her breath as she balanced trying to put the clasps back on the grinder. She worked hard to hold in her vomit as she tried to make it look like nothing was out of place.

As quietly as possible, she reconnected the grinder door and pushed it underneath the shelf. She could hear footsteps echoing as she looked around, trying desperately to find a place to hide. That's when she saw them. The coffins. Two empties… one occupied.

"Oh my God." *I have to do it. It's for the story.* It's the lengths she was willing to go to. *It's the only way to get the story.*

Climbing in felt otherworldly. Most people never experience being in a coffin. That was much after postmortem, long after life passed out of your body. There was no time to think about it now as the steps came closer. That's when she realized she had forgotten to turn the lights off. *It's too late now.* She quickly laid down and closed the coffin's lid.

It was like being shoved into a tightly fitting closet. There was no room to even roll onto her side. Her breathing was shallow and became more rushed. Claustrophobia set in, and she could feel the panic creep up her body. A scream welled up from deep within her body, but she found a way to suppress it. *I can't get caught!* Sweat beaded on her forehead as she desperately tried to control her breathing. Lying there listening, she could hear the steps enter the room and stop.

Everything was silent. Time stopped. All she could see were small cracks of light peeking through the coffin lid.

The steps started again. She could hear the person moving stuff around, no doubt checking things out. *I'm sure they're trying to see what was out of place and why the light was on.* Susan just tried to hold still.

With each shuffle, the steps seemed to come increasingly closer. Her mind's eye imagined Johnny's tall form walking patiently around, trying to find the intruder. She pushed away thoughts of what he would do if he found her.

Fertilizer for the Sunflowers.

Her head shook involuntarily with the thought. *Shit! Did I say that out loud?* She froze in place.

Now, the steps were right outside her coffin. She panicked.

Clink-clink. It sounded like Johnny may have found her.

"Susan?" A whisper broke through the silence. Except it wasn't a testosterone-lowered voice. Instead, it was the voice of a woman.

Ashleigh.

A wave of relief washed over her, and she pushed on the coffin's lid. It didn't move. She tried again a little harder.

Nothing.

"Ashleigh," her voice echoed in the box. "I'm in here, but the door is stuck."

"You're in the coffin?"

"Yes." Panic rushed over her again as she started pushing harder. "Help me get out of here."

"Did you get the pictures you needed?"

Jesus, that is hardly important right now.

"Yes, I found the meat grinder, some blood, and a tooth. Now please, I'm freaking out here."

"God, you really will go to any length to get your story, won't you?" Ashleigh mocked her.

"Help me out now, Ashleigh. This isn't funny."

"I actually had a question for you first. Be honest, and I will open the coffin."

Susan was mortified. *What the hell is this lady's issue?*

"Does the name Hamscombe mean anything to you?"

Hands now clenched into fists, Susan began banging on the door. *Hamscombe? Nothing off the top of her head.* She could barely think.

"No."

"Really think hard about this. How about a Steven Hamscombe?"

That was a name she hadn't heard in many years. Steven Hamscombe. Her first big story. He was a procurement VP for a public works company. To save money, he replaced the city's drinking water pipes with cheap, non-Galvanized pipes. Lead had become an issue. Last she remembered, he was rotting in a prison somewhere.

"I seem to recall someone with that name, but I might be able to think better if I wasn't lying in a coffin!" At the end of her statement, her voice rose a few decibels.

"I'm glad you remembered him. Obviously, you didn't recognize me. My last name used to be Hamscombe, too, you know."

Susan's heart sank.

"Steven and I had just celebrated six years when he was arrested."

"Okay, fine. Steven was a scumbag. You deserved someone better. Do you know how many people got sick because of him? I helped put a bad person away. You are better off without him."

"Yes, and you got your big break, didn't you? That made you very famous. Then I read about your last fiasco. You know, that story brought a big smile to my face. It turns out you never truly get the story all the way right. Do you?"

"Look, Ashleigh. You might blame me for messing up your life, but that doesn't change what Steve did." She called him Steve. Like she had in the past.

"It turns out you weren't right about Steven either. He never made the call about the pipes. That was done before he took the job. In fact, he was hired to quietly fix the pipes. The company knew about the lead. Steven worked to replace them with safe options, but you missed that.”

“That’s not true. Steve tried to plead that same story in court, but the documents said otherwise.”

“Steven,” she put a heavy emphasis on the *-en*. “Was never good at pillow talk. I suppose you didn’t have to do much convincing once you opened your legs.

“Steve and I never.”

“I told you to be honest!” Ashleigh slammed her fist on top of the coffin.

Of course, Susan was lying, but what was she supposed to say? *Yes, I slept with your husband. Yes, he was a lousy lay and most of the time fell asleep right after?* That would certainly calm her down.

“You know,” Ashleigh’s voice was calm again. “I wasn’t lying about what this funeral home is doing. That’s the funny part about this whole situation. I’m going to leave you in here, and you’ll be the first body buried in that cemetery. An actual occupied coffin.” Ashleigh laughed manically.

Susan screamed at her. She tossed out obscenities and slammed her palms on the coffin to no avail.

“Hey, Susan,” Ashleigh giggled, “I have an exclusive for you.” Her hands swept through the air as if reading a theatre marquee. “Investigative reporter buried alive in bodiless cemetery. What do you think? Is that headline news?”

"Ashleigh, is everything alright in here?" A deeper voice asked. "I noticed the lights on while I was driving by."

It was Johnny. Susan began to scream *let me out* and *help*.

"Oh my god, is someone in there?" Heavy steps approached the coffin.

"Yes, please, it's Susan, from the tour earlier."

"Why are you in that coffin?"

"Because that crazy bitch locked me in here. Please help me!" Susan pleaded.

"She's a reporter." Ashleigh cut in. "An investigative reporter."

"Oh my. I see," Johnny confirmed. "Did you see anything?" He patted the coffin's lid.

"No, I swear." She sounded desperate. "Even if I did, I would say nothing."

"I caught her taking pictures," Ashleigh again cut in.

"Oh boy."

"Listen, Johnny. Please, I'm begging you. Let me out, and I'll leave this town, and you'll never see me again. There will be no story. This will never surface."

"You promise?" Johnny asked.

"I swear on my mother's grave," Susan retorted.

A laugh broke out between Johnny and Ashleigh.

"No pun intended, I'm sure. Alright, since you promised."

She heard Johnny's hand jiggling something on the coffin, and then he paused.

No, no, come on!

"You know. Tomorrow, the judges are coming for the sunflowers. It would be really bad timing if this were to get out. You'd be surprised at how great humans are as fertilizer. In a way, we're just giving back to nature, after all."

"Please. Ashleigh, I'm so sorry for what I did to you. I promise I will go back and contest Steve's sentence. Johnny, no one will ever know. You can just keep going as if I never came here. I'll even give you my camera!"

Alas, no matter how much pleading or begging she did, Johnny nor Ashleigh ever responded. After a while, her voice gave out, and so did her body. She could barely move a muscle. The last thing she heard was the sound of Earth piling on top of wood. It was deafening.

****

A newspaper hit the front doorstep of the funeral home as the sun surfaced, breaking the plane of the Earth. Johnny grabbed it and opened it up. The first page read: *Overisel Wins Best Flower Town for the 12th Year*. The bottom right had a blurb. It was aptly titled *Tom VanOlmstead Remembered*. The article mentioned how he would be missed by his wife, two children, and loving niece.

TERROR BELOW GROUND

"Oh great, here she comes, guys," she heard a man say as she watched him lick chocolate off his fat digits.

Headphones were not yet in her ears. That wouldn't come until she entered the crime scene. She surveyed every detail with each step. She saw Detective Shehan with his belly emerging from his khaki trench coat. The fedora sat stained and dirty on his head over his wet, messy hair. She dared not think of the condition of it, lest her stomach turned. To his right were three beat cops who looked like puppies begging for attention from their master. They were in blue uniforms, prim and proper. It was quite the contrast from the uncouth, disheveled detective before them. Yet, for some reason, that is what they idolized?

Green, wet, and slimy. Each step down the subway stairs into the lower levels was an inner-city hell. It smelled dank and musty. Graffiti tags marked the walls with their urban art. She saw the form of a nude woman pass on her left. In contrast to her own, the breasts were quite full, with yellow spray-painted nipples. It made her feel rather uncomfortable.

She was pretty in her own right, though. Commanding a presence with her almost six-foot frame. She didn't have much in the way of curves, but she was fit. With a strict diet and an exercise regimen that would make most people shake their heads in wonder, she kept a nice womanly figure. It was her height that caused issues with the men in her life. That, with her lack of skills in interpersonal relationships, kept her single. Her strawberry blonde hair was tucked into a bun high up on her head. She wore a professional blouse with tactical khaki pants. Her light parcel sack hung over her shoulder instead of a purse. Everything was neat and in place on purpose. Her badge sat proudly on her chest lapel, stating, *Detective Bauer.*

Detective Shehan approached her at the bottom of the stairs and held out his recently licked fingers for a handshake. He smiled, baring his neglected teeth.

Bauer looked down. Blinked slowly, then looked back to his face. She did not offer her hand in return. The thought was unbearable.

"Detective Shehan," she said with a nod.

"Hello, Elizabeth," he grunted while tucking his hand into his coat pocket, a bit offended.

"It's Detective Bauer."

"Right, sorry," he knew she preferred the formal title, but he didn't have much respect for her. Truth be told, she made him feel insignificant and insecure. Quickly trying to cover it up, he began again, "Some poor vagrant was run over by a subway train. Damn drifter probably OD'd on the tracks when…"

"Shut it," Elizabeth's tone remained consistent; it didn't rise or get louder. "I don't want to know anything. I just want to see it myself. I don't need anyone throwing me off by giving me their theory, so please stop."

The beat cops' jaws dropped at how she spoke to Shehan. They didn't like the guy, but if you wanted to get off the beat someday, you needed connections to move up. Shehan demanded a lot of praise and did not put up with being spoken to that way.

"Right again, sorry," he said, his face turning as red as a ripe tomato in a summer garden. He was pissed, but the Captain kept Detective Bauer for special cases. She had an impeccable record and found things no one else ever did. She was peculiar and strict with her practices. The men in the department all joked about some sort of PMS hocus pocus. When she wasn't around, of course. One time, Shehan witnessed her take down another detective almost twice her weight on the mat. He taunted her, and she gladly accepted the challenge. After that, no one ever messed with her again. "Please do your thing."

"I will." Reaching in her pockets, she pulled out her earbuds and then looked back. "Make sure the blues don't come and mess anything up in my crime scene. Forensics will be here shortly."

Now, the beat cops were offended. Mess anything up? They knew better. One stepped up to say something, but Shehan stopped him.

"Don't," he said. "Captain says to let her do her thing." He paused to make sure her buds were in, and she could no longer hear him. "T;ween you and me, she's autistic or something. However, she gets shit done."

"Jesus… really?" the officer replied. *Crate* was the name on his badge.

"Yah, really. Just watch."

Metal music filled Elizabeth's ears as she closed her eyes. This blocked the world around her and shut everything out. She forgot about Shehan and the blue uniforms standing beside him. She forgot about the people crowding the yellow police tape. The slime reporters trying to get the first scoop. All of that noise, that business, was gone.

Slowly, she opened her eyes to view the crime scene again in a new light. It truly was a different experience. Slamming distorted guitars with a bass line reverberating in her ears, and the repetitive kick of the double bass with the snare drum roll buried the world. It shut out the hum, and it was like she switched her vision to a mode honed in on details, small clues others rarely noticed.

As she walked closer, she could see that the caboose of the subway was stopped part of the way across the platform. It stopped almost instantly. *As instantly as a 40-mph train can stop along the tracks.* She could still smell bits of the brake friction in the air. It was the strong aroma of metal upon metal. As she approached the edge of the platform, she finally saw the vic's body in full sight. It was segmented. Half a body on one side of the track and the other half below. The lower half was a few feet further forward than the top half; *most likely due to the tumbling of the body beneath the train cars as it ran over the man.* Red pulpy liquid splay across the tracks. She recalled her first scene and how she wanted to vomit from these sights, but she had grown accustomed.

Every mortician had the same joke whenever she brought in bodies. "They're dying to see me." Her eyes rolled.

Looking past the pulpy red, she could tell right away that this was no drifter, as Shehan had so delicately suggested. *This man, or whatever is left of him, had decent clothes. No signs of dirt or unusual wear and tear.* She could tell even from this distance that he had a well-manicured hairstyle. *Nothing extravagant, but most definitely a recent cut.* Not only that, she could tell that his face was clean-shaven, and recently so.

She lowered herself to the track level. It was a good five-foot drop. The metal track was in its winding crescendo, nearing the end. A finger-tapping solo outro played with a long and impressive scream from the singer. Her long frame landed well, and she showed little to no difficulty getting down there. A thought passed through her mind of Shehan climbing down. *I doubt he even tried.*

Now was the part she preferred; time to get up close and personal with the victim. With one long wail of the guitar, the track ended. The next song began, but this one started with the slow hum of a cello. It was an orchestral piece. This was her method. She didn't know why it worked, but it did. With each music change, she entered into a different state of vision. It was a jarring transition from such a hard metal track. This transition was intentional. Her whole playlist was laid out this way. As an investigator, you had to keep a fresh mind and, even more importantly, fresh eyes. Her mind allowed the jarring transition, and she began to focus on the smaller, more personal clues.

Studying the ground as she walked, she picked out some inconsistencies. Still, she did not want to make assumptions based on anything yet. She noticed that some of the stones had been disturbed in a way inconsistent with a man falling off a platform. They were misplaced, and it almost appeared to be a track. Two actually. However, the stones by the track caused disruption as they were scattered by the intense vibrations from the train car. *Was this correlated? Too little information to tell.*

Next was the body. The lower half was mangled and several feet away from the torso due to being run over. This was not ideal, for visual clues would likely have been indiscernible from the trauma. She continued to look over the body as a melodic violin took the lead melody, playing harmoniously in her ear. It was still loud enough to block out the rabble of whispering beat cops, and civilian rubberneckers.

Just as she had thought, the bloodied lower half was in disarray. *Rips and tears in the once pristine jeans in several areas.* It was in a weird non-human position. However, her earlier observations led her to investigate in a much more pointed direction. She looked at the feet. One foot still had a shoe on, but the other lay with just a sock. *Where was the missing shoe? Could it have been launched? Carried along with the train?*

Jutting up like a prairie dog from the ground, she looked left and right along the track. Her head swung wildly. She saw no visual of the missing shoe. She whipped out her flashlight and shined it below the train car. *Nothing.* She looked back toward the tunnel. *Nothing.* She took out a tool to observe one more thing on the body. The bottom of the pants where they would rest on the man's heels. *There is definite wear and tear.* However, was it enough to envelope the narrative forming in her mind? She had to be right. She needed to be specific. This type of claim is not one made of assumptions. She needed to make sure her bias didn't impede the evidence.

Time to examine the torso.

A refrain played in her ears, carried out by the percussion. The snare snapped to a beat accompanied by the xylophone. Eventually, each instrument would join. She could hear the French horn with its unusual sound leading to the next chorus. Soon, the conclusion.

Elizabeth now studied the poor man's face. His innards had all been laid out. She knew that the man had been run over, but there was something else. Confirming her earlier suspicions, the man was most definitely not a drifter. He wasn't particularly handsome, but he wasn't run down nor showed physical evidence of being a user. Despite the trauma, his short black hair maintained some semblance of being styled with a side part. *Eyes open with a glassy stare, amber highlighting his brown eyes.* It was as if he was staring at her, mouthing '*help me.*'

"I will," she reassured him. Of course, even she couldn't hear her own voice.

He was wearing a red flannel shirt with a white, now stained red, undershirt. Suddenly she wished he could turn him over, but the crime scene techs were still on their way. *They will need the pictures.* As the music began to wrap into its final whirring fadeout, she caught it. His collar was all the way up by the bottom of his jaw. In fact, the sides appeared to touch his ears. She looked even closer; the music swelled to the outro, and she confirmed it.

This man was murdered.

The drag marks in the stones. The wear and tear on the bottom of his jeans. The missing shoe. Now, the flannel. This man was being dragged across the tracks, obviously in a hurry. However, the murderer was far too late. Her mind reconstructed the murderer pulling with all his or her might. Flannel gripped in their hands at the shoulders, pulling him across the tracks as they realized the train was coming. They hurried but to no avail.

Was he dead before this, or just incapacitated? That was a question for later.

Bum, dah, bummmm!

The music went from a crescendo to its finale!

What of the murderer?

Electronic noises began in her ears. Another jarring transition. She recalled this was the theme of a video game she played when she was younger. The techno sounds of synthesizers ran in her ears, rearranging her brain like fruits being put together in a basket for a housewarming gift.

Now, she diverted her attention to any means of escape. *Where would the murderer go?* She looked up. She saw a door on the other side up on the ramp. It read *Mechanical Room.* No exit sign above it. *Would he be dumb enough to go back up where the people waited?*

She scanned the area again. *No. There would've been reports of a man covered in blood. There is no way he left that unscathed. He was likely showered in the victim's blood. It would have exploded like a ripe peach in summertime. The only place was down either side of the tunnel.*

Elizabeth wasted no time. She went to the wall. *He would've been in a hurry.* With the beeps and boops filling her ears, she looked at every brick along the wall. Anything giving her the impression of which way he went. She continued to walk until she saw it. It was faint, but it was there. *Blood.*

She used a cotton swap and tucked it in an evidence tube. She kept them in her pocket just for occasions like this. Normal women her age kept lipstick or cover-up. Not her. This was her life. She dabbed at it. It was tiny. Less than the size of a marble. It could've been paint for all she knew. *There is only one way to tell.*

With calculated pressure, she dabbed the red on the brick. When she pulled it off, she looked at the tip of the cotton swab. It was red. *Boom! Score!* Other detectives mocked her for this, but she took a magnifying glass out of her pocket. It was straight out of Sherlock Holmes, but today was the day to use it. She hovered it over the red and noticed a pattern. *It's a swipe.* She poured luminal into the glass vial and then inserted the second cotton swab. Once again, pulling out her flashlight, she set it to black light. She mixed the vial and illuminated it.

Instant results. Man, the modern age is fun. It's blood.

Ripping the earbuds out of her ears, she ran back to the side of the loading platform. The killer was likely still in the tunnels, and they could be hiding, just waiting to get out. They had one chance to find them.

"Shehan," she called, waiving her hands to get her pear-shaped colleague's attention.

Breathing heavily as he walked, he rolled his eyes and wondered if she caught that. *Doubt it with how far she was.* Reaching the edge, he could see the seriousness in her face.

"What is it Elizabe…" he stopped himself, "Detective Bauer?"

"I need your two men over there. Crate and the other guy," she pointed.

Shehan was actually impressed; she was observant. She knew the guy who stepped up and had read his badge. He turned back to the Blues, gave a whistle, and urged them over with a hand signal.

As Elizabeth looked around, she saw a maintenance guy working on a control box further up on the platform near the crowd. *Must've been called in when the train car made an emergency stop.*

"You there," she called out to him.

At first, he didn't turn.

"Maintenance guy," she yelled a little louder.

Shehan motioned to Crate to grab the maintenance man. He seemed genuinely surprised and a bit nervous as Crate spoke a few words and then urged him over.

"What's up Bauer?" Shehan pressed.

Before answering, she waited to make sure everyone was present.

"This is not a suicide or an OD. This is now a murder scene. Shehan, I need you to call it in."

"What… how did you…" he began to ask.

"There's no time. I have reason to believe that the murderer went back down the tunnel that way. You Sir; what's your name?"

"Who, me?" The maintenance guy was bewildered. Likely shocked at hearing the word murder. He looked at the body and then looked away quickly. "The name's Earl."

"Earl, how far is the next station?" she asked quickly pointing to her right. It was the tunnel she deduced the murderer escaped into.

"Oh, I suppose it's about six or seven miles," he scratched his ratty hair. He had the appearance of someone who worked mostly in the dark and away from people. The man was late middle-aged. Brown curly hair hugged the edges of his receding hairline. Unkempt facial hair adorned his face. It looked like it had been a while since he had looked in the mirror or appeared in public. He wore an orange safety vest with reflector tape over the top of a blue mechanic's jumpsuit.

Brown muddy work boots hung below the blue pants.

Elizabeth thought he was exactly what she would expect a subway technician to look like.

"Crate and..." she peered at the other badge; "ah, Weber. I need you with me. Shehan, call in the murder and get back up. There is no way that the killer has made it to the other station. Just in case, have dispatch send officers there and tell them to watch the tunnel. Boys, we're going in." Crate and Weber nodded.

"Excuse me, Miss?" Earl asked as Crate and Weber jumped not so gingerly down to the tracks.

"What is it, Earl?"

"Well, I've worked these tunnels for the past twenty years, see, and it's just that...." He wrenched his hands together nervously. "It's just that there are a lot of alcoves, pockets, and even other tunnels that used to have some purpose but don't anymore."

"Go on. What's your point," she asked as the two officers got their flashlights and firearms out.

"My point is that, well, if someone really went in there, this murderer... he could be hiding in a good many places. Also, it's really easy to get lost. One wrong turn and radios half the time don't work or nothing."

"Okay then. That's a damn fine point. Who knows these tunnels besides you? Anyone here?"

"No. Like I said, I've been working nights here for going on two decades now."

"Then it's settled. We're taking you with us," Elizabeth said. She didn't notice that the men's bodies all went stiff simultaneously and looked at her like she was crazy.

"Excuse me, ma'am? I ain't got no gun or nothing like that." Earl's body language tightened up, and he squirmed where he stood.

"Don't worry, you won't need it. We'll just need you to show us these areas where he could potentially be hiding. We won't ask you to do anything you're not comfortable with. Besides, you'll be with uniformed officers the whole time."

Shehan shook his head and a laugh escaped from his gut. He walked away. There was no way he was going in that damned tunnel. He decided to walk so he could deny having any involvement in this. He muttered, *crazy bitch,* under his breath. At this point, he didn't care if she heard him.

If she had heard it, she gave no indication. Earl dropped down to the Track level. For him, it was a calculated move, one that looked natural since he had done it so many times before.

"Crate, I need you with Earl. Make sure you cover him. Get your flashlights out and weapons ready. There is no knowing where this perp could be hiding out. If we get to the next station without finding him along the way, then he might have eluded us, but at least we tried."

Both Crate and Weber nodded acknowledgment. They were impressed with her stern speech and in-control manner. This was something they had not expected. Her confidence gave them confidence, and they suddenly felt much better about the whole situation.

"Ma'am, I won't let Earl leave my side," Crate responded, noting her beauty. He hadn't really noticed it before.

"I'm also ready. We should move quickly as there is no telling how far he went." Weber looked at everyone. He was pumped. The adrenaline had already begun coursing through his veins like the effect a few shots of whiskey has in a man: liquid courage.

"Earl, you ready? You're our map." Elizabeth waited for a response.

Earl fumbled with his hands and awkwardly grabbed his flashlight. Nerves had taken over, and he was visibly shaken. Clumsily, he flipped on his large flashlight, which had four bulbs in the end and was the color of a safety cone. It was obviously designed for blue-collar purposes.

"Yes, I suppose I am," he didn't make eye contact with a single person.

Each step felt weighted and strange. The loose rocks fumbled beneath their shoes with each step, making each one difficult. It wasn't long before their lights beamed through the dark tunnel like spotlights over a diner reminding people to *eat at Joe's* or like a red-carpet gala meant only for the wealthy and influential. They had now entered the tunnel, like rats in a maze. Elizabeth pondered the question… *If we are the rats, then are we seeking out the cat?*

Minutes passed with no trace of where the perp had gone. So far, they saw only straight tunnels with walls on either side. It had almost immediately curved to the right, and every step seemed like a never-ending turn. They thought that soon they'd be right back where they started.

"It's not long now," Earl's whisper sounded like a yell as the echobounced off the walls.

"Not long 'til what?" Crate's reverberating whisper answered.

"Than we come onto side tunnels, old maintenance halls, and abandoned rooms. I find a lot of squatters in here. They're pretty harmless, but I still have to kick them out."

"I'll move ahead then," Elizabeth signaled with her hand to stay back; she was barely visible in the darkness. "Crate, you and Earl take the center, and Weber, you follow on the rear. I don't want anyone getting the jump on us."

"Affirmative," Weber responded eagerly. He didn't seem to have much personality, but he certainly lived for excitement like this.

They all remained silent and listened with hitched breath for any sound that gave way to someone being present. It made sense. *The killer likely would wait for a few hours, let things cool down, then head out the way he came in.* Elizabeth's mind tracked the logic. *He'd wait at one of the stations and disappear into the faceless crowd of passersby, waiting for their subway trains.*

Illuminated by the yellow of the flashlight, Elizabeth found the first side tunnel. It was dimly lit and looked like it had received little to no maintenance over the last decade, maybe more. Crumbling stones in the archway and flecked paint were the tell-tale signs. Then, she was hit with the smell. A memory flashed of the police locker room outside the gym. It was a wet body odor, a combination of sweat and poor hygiene.

"Earl," Elizabeth raised her hand to signal a halt. "What's down there?"

"Shit, um, it's an old maintenance hall with a couple of rooms. We switched out controls near the track. Probably got some vagrants."

"In detail. I need to know how many rooms and in what direction. Be specific." Her hand grazed the pocket that her headphones hid in. It was her comfort. Her mind had already begun spinning. She didn't even notice this habit.

"You heard her Earl," Crate bumped Earl with his shoulder. Again, always ready to make a good impression.

"Alright. About ten yards in, it splits from left to right. To the left, it's about twenty yards to an empty room. Maybe some trash or empty bottles. To the right used to be a power station. It's a ways back, about another thirty yards. It's a large room, again, still empty." Earl could sense the agitation in his voice, but slowly, he cooled down as he explained.

"Damn." Elizabeth inched closer to the entrance. "Weber radio this in."

With a whirring, he asked for a copy on the walkie on his chest. Silence was the only reply.

"Radios don't work for nothing down here," Earl responded in a told-you-so sort of way.

"I can't get anyone, Detective," Weber said.

"Okay, let's go in, but carefully. Weber, you come with me to the far room. Crate, take Earl, but make sure he doesn't enter that room until it is clear. Remember your training officers. Yell if you find someone and keep your weapon ready. We're potentially cornering a coyote. He could be desperate and gnashing." Her imagery with her words was strong. It's not how detectives usually spoke, but she wasn't just any detective.

They confirmed her command. Crate walked and used his hand to cover Earl and file him away behind him as they went to the left. Elizabeth felt that if the murderer was hiding here, it would likely be in the farther room. *Less likely to be found. Or he could pass off as a vagrant.* She nodded to Crate as they parted ways.

Elizabeth and Weber walked slowly and deliberately down the hall, but it was obvious that Earl was right; it only went to one destination. There was no doorway, just an open rectangle where a door maybe once hung but for years had not. She saw a pile of trash right past the threshold. In the same motion, they both raised their weapons, walking in tandem. She certainly hoped that Weber knew how to clear a room.

The smell grew worse the closer they got to the door.

They stopped at the entrance and looked at each other. When ready, they both nodded and popped in. Elizabeth went to the left, and Weber went straight in. They tried to illuminate every end of the room. Suddenly, she illuminated a body lying slumped on the floor.

"Crate! Over here!"

They approached slowly together, regrouping.

"You there, do not move!" Weber yelled, aiming at the body.

There was no response and no movement.

"Answer me now!"

Elizabeth looked at Weber, and they cautiously approached. With the tip of her foot, she nudged the body. It shifted with her movement but held no reaction. Concerned, she directed Weber to flip the body as she locked on with her gun.

"Don't do anything stupid. We are the police. We have guns aimed. I will not hesitate to shoot."

Still no response.

Weber slowly turned the body toward them and backed away in disgust. It was just a shell of a man. Literally. This man's body was gutted. A hole gaped from the bottom of his sternum to the base of his pelvis. All of the insides had been removed. No stomach, intestines, lungs… nothing. It appeared to be a fleshy husk, like cows hanging on butcher's hooks.

Weber uttered something guttural and backed away several feet, trying to hold back the vomit.

Elizabeth barely reacted. Her light held steady, illuminating the poor vagrant. She could see his vertebrae shining through. From the bodies she'd seen, she guessed that this man was dead maybe a week or two. *No way to know for sure, but the browning around the muscle and the flies suggestsit. The smell is horrid, but it could be worse.*

Then, she noticed something at the edge of her flashlight. *Supplies.*

"Weber, look at this."

Wiping his mouth from either salivating or actually puking, he returned, not quite ready to look again.

In the luminance of the flashlight was a roll of black trash bags and a used pile of duct tape. Her light followed this trail to a wall and lit up what appeared to be dozens of black bags, all full to the brim.

"What the actual fu…" but Weber's words were cut off with a scream. It sounded like Crate.

They both ran back without a second thought. Each step was menacing, and the cool underground air hurt their lungs.

Soon, they were through the hall back on their way across the fork. Elizabeth saw Earl first. He was huddled into a ball on the ground outside the room. She knelt down and waved Weber forward. Weber stormed into the room.

"Earl, are you okay?" Her hand touched his shoulder, and he writhed like a startled worm.

He kept saying something, but it wasn't understandable.

"Weber, what's going on?"

"Detective Bauer, we have a serious problem!" He hobbled out with Crate in his arms. The officer had his hand holding Crate's throat.

"Oh my God, get him into the tunnel now!"

Once out in the open, Elizabeth commanded Weber to find a signal and get them support and evac units. Weber wandered everywhere, testing his radio until he got a signal. She did her best to dress Crate's wound. It was a cut to his neck, and she prayed it wasn't his jugular. When she removed his hand, she could see that the penetration was jagged and was likely not made from a knife.

Crate was not in good condition. He kept pointing down the tunnel. Earl walked back and forth, swearing and saying things like *I shouldn't be here* and *I'm no cop*. Luckily, Elizabeth always kept a first aid kit in her parcel sack, and she could provide a pressure cloth, but it was only temporary. "We need those medics!" That's when Weber came back.

"I've got them. They are on their way. It should only be a minute or two." Weber knelt beside Crate. "Hang in there, buddy; we'll get this son of bitch."

Crate again just pointed down the tunnel. Earl was still losing it. He was in the way of where Crate was pointing, and they looked down the tunnel.

The killer must've run down this way. Elizabeth wished Crate could speak.

Distantly down the tunnel, they could see the lights from the medic crew. Small circular tubes of lights flashed their way into this dark hell they now traversed.

The guy we're after is no one-time killer. Now ,Elizabeth understood. *The body or bodies in the other room were part of this guy's modus operandum.*

She held Crate's hand to his throat.

"Please hold on," Elizabeth pleaded. Her eyes were distant; almost like she was speaking to someone else. Someone not in this room. "They are close. I can see them from here. They're going to take care of you. You're going to be okay." God, she hoped so.

With a longing to stay, she let go. This man was her responsibility, but she owed it to him to find his killer as well as those dead already who beckoned to her. *Avenge me!* They screamed.

"Weber, we need to move if we're going to bring this guy in."

"What about Crate?"

"I can see the paramedics on the way. I need you to snap Earl out of it. We need to push on. I cannot let this guy get away." Elizabeth now knew it was most definitely a man. *The size of those men and the weight of them. The way he got Crate.* That was more consistent with what a man would or could do based on her training and experience.

"Earl, what is down there?" Weber wasn't pleasant. He grabbed Earl by the collar and held him close. Weber pointed down the tunnel. He was not happy. In fact, he was pissed. No one messed with his partner or anyone else close to him.

Crate was very upset but soon passed out. Elizabeth was making a tough call. She wasn't comfortable with it, but she felt it was necessary. She let Crate go. She grabbed Earl and turned him.

"You need to guide us. I know you're scared. I know you're uncomfortable, but no one gets away with this. Do you understand?" Inches from Earl's face, she pushed on him.

"Yes." It was quiet but audible. "This continues, but then splits. One side goes to an old section of track. The other is the modern track."

"Then we go and fast." Elizabeth pushed both Earl and Weber to move.

They began to move at a fast pace. She constantly looked behind her to ensure that she made the right choice. Soon, Crate was surrounded by other lights. Then, she could no longer see them as the tunnel walls swallowed her vision.

Minutes passed. They didn't see any other person ahead of them. Still, they pushed forward. That's when they saw it. The tracks separated in a "Y" pattern. There were left and right choices, again.

"Earl," Elizabeth stopped, catching her breath, and the other two were thankful for the break. "What lies in each direction?"

With labored breath, he answered. "To your left leads to the next station. To the right is an abandoned part of the track that has been retired for years. It used to go to the central city station but no longer."

"What is it with this place. It's a maze." Elizabeth began to feel overwhelmed, but she had worked on this.

"What's the plan boss?" Weber asked deliberately.

"Weber, take Earl to the next station. I'm going to explore this old part of the tracks."

"I wouldn't advise that," Earl tried to warn.

"Why?"

"This part of the track doesn't go anywhere; it's a dead end." Earl seemed to regain his cool.

"Then he won't have a place to go." Elizabeth looked on in confidence.

The party once again split. She lifted her walkie, signaling that if Weber found something, he should call. Silently, he nodded.

"Good luck, Bauer. I will see you on the other side." Weber said.

Earl looked uneasy as he watched her trail away down the old stretch of railway.

The tracks aren't always placed in the way you should want them to be. Sometimes, the tracks tell you where to go. Destiny can deal an ugly hand when you least expect it. Especially that of a detective. It was her job to bring the bad guy to justice. She questioned everything at this point. The direction, her assessment, but she was right up to this point. Why would she stop here? *It's my job to question things.*

With that boost of confidence, she moved on. She followed the tracks away from her support. Weber's flashlight soon disappeared from her vision, and she entered a world created years earlier. *This section looks untouched for decades.* She looked around and took note of the green moss growing on the slate walls and floor. She wondered what this may have looked like in its heyday. *It was a glorious marble wonder where people would look in awe as they passed it. Soon to be forgotten by a new subway entrance. One more attractive to the workers and residents.*

Tall ceilings made it feel like a cave she was spelunking, rediscovering an old relic many humans had forgotten. A religious sacrament that people once held as their sanctuary. *The first person who cared to take in the gathering.* Moss-grown slate stone with its 1980s aesthetics. *A time forgotten in space. The world moved on without it.*

Elizabeth noticed a shack in the middle of the area. It was the only thing lit by a bulb. It stuck out like a sore thumb in comparison. She approached carefully, already suspicious. Her mind played the heavy drums of the metal music she heard earlier. *Is this my time? If it is, am I ready?*

"Is anyone there?" Her voice echoed with no answer.

The shack sat alone. It was a cube lit of fluorescent fixtures giving an offsetting glow. As she approached it, it did not seem abandoned. No dust, no rust, nothing that would normally push her over the edge of deceit. It seemed like a modern installment in an aged area. With care, she approached.

A click reverberated in the air as she entered. It was a cheap plastic door like from a front porch. The door swung with a slam behind her as the spring pulled it shut. With the sudden slam, she turned just to be reassured she was alone. *This is not an abandoned station. The computer is from the later 2010s.* There was a sense that even though the rest of this area was forgotten, this small portion maintained the time.

It was a six-foot by six-foot cube where she could see only a couple of lockers surrounding an aged computer screen. As she turned to the lockers, she questioned everything she saw. With her thumb, she lifted the latch, and the metal wrung open with a *ting*.

Gasp!

Before her hung a maintenance outfit covered in blood with maintenance shoes also bloody on the bottom of the locker. The oval patch with graceful blue script read *Earl* on a white background. *It was right in front of me the whole time.* Even Crate pointed it out to her, but her hubris denied it. She was great at reading crime scenes, but she was not great at reading people. The killer was leading them down this tunnel the whole time.

With a speed faster than her mind, she whipped the walkie-talkie to her mouth and radioed for Weber. All she got back was static. There was no one on the other end. Like the radio, her mind was filled with static noise. *Either I don't have a signal, or worse, Weber is already dead.*

Bang!

Dropping the radio and retrieving her gun, she spun toward the shack door. Something slammed into it. With calculated steps, she looked for any other entrance. There was another door in the back of the cube, but she didn't see anyone in that glass either. In front of her, however, there was a smear of red. *A splatter. Blood.* She didn't need any chemicals to tell her that.

Pressing the latch, it released, and to her surprise, it was an empty, vast space. *Nothing there but the echoes of times past.* Then she noticed it. Before her, on the dark ground, lay what appeared to be a wallet. She crouched, still holding her weapon ready. She flipped open the wallet with her free hand. The leather was surprisingly warm… and wet.

It wasn't a wallet. It was a badge. *WEBER. It'sWeber's badge.* "Shit!" She let go of the badge, jumped out of the shack, and put her back against the wall, feeling the cold steel through her clothes.

Laughter erupted, filling the tunnels as she fumbled for her flashlight. She rested her gun hand on her flashlight and shone it in every direction.

"Earl? You out there?" Her breaths became deeper as she worked to calm her racing heart.

"So, you found it, I suppose. Good! You know it has been a long time coming. Finally, I can be appreciated for my art." The voice echoed in all directions. It sounded like Earl but different. Something much more menacing, like a darkness had crept inside his voice, lowering it a few octaves.

"Where's Officer Weber, Earl?" She learned in class about humanizing the target. *Use his name. Personalize your messages.*

"I suppose it was a matter of time. I got antsy. The mayor was *cleaning* up the city, so there have been fewer vagrants down here lately. I had to continue my art, you see." Again, his voice quadrupled in its echo.

No way to find the source.

"Anyway, what good is art if you don't have anyone to appreciate it?"

"Earl," she needed to think carefully through her next words. "I didn't see your art. I just found your bloody uniform. Why don't you come out? You can show it to me."

"Damn," silence persisted for a moment. "That's funny. I guess I was in such a hurry. I just needed to change clothes so I could answer the maintenance call. After all, no one knows these tunnels like me."

"Earl."

"Shut up! Do you hear it?"

"Hear what?"

"The symphony. It's almost complete. I've made so many before, but this one… This one is special. It must be how Van Goo, or whatever his name is, felt." There was a shuffling of feet. "It's on the wall adjacent to the old station. Hidden just enough to allow my work to be completed without interruption. Now, the smell. That was hard to hide, but I found ways."

Elizabeth thought back to the symphony she had just listened to. *Is this the overture or the finale?* She couldn't hear any symphony. *Doesn't matter. I've got to find Earl.* That's what matters.

"Earl, I don't see it. Where is it?"

A flashlight beam suddenly flashed, illuminating a wall of red entrails placed into the form of a naked woman. It was shiny like some kind of polish was sprayed over it. This was all Elizabeth's mind could process as she ran from her hiding place. The source of the light was what she needed.

A ghastly white face winced as her flashlight caught Earl in its beam. His eyes became slits. Immediately, He was her target. The smell of sulfur filled the air as the sound deafened her ears with every trigger pull. She watched Earl's body contract with each bullet that hit her target. His body fell backward. All she remembered was his mouth gaping wide. *Was he screaming?* She didn't know. It happened in less than five seconds, but felt like hours. Then, the overstimulation. Her ears rang. Everything became blurry. His body was on the ground.

She pushed through to make sure he was indeed down. Earl didn't appear to have a weapon.

Remember what your therapist said. She fell onto her butt and began rocking. She covered her ears with her hands. Her mind was split into a million pieces. Finally, a piece began independent thought, bringing her hand down to her earbuds. Quickly grabbing them and shoving them into her ears, she scrambled for her phone, trembling. Desperately, she pressed play, and a rock song began.

It was a rock ballad. The mix of singing and screaming soothed her soul. Slowly, with every beat of the bass and snap of the snare, she began to rebuild the puzzle of her mind.

After that, she didn't remember much before blacking out. Now, the music filled her as her mind hit reset.

****

Opening her eyes, she smelled something so pungent and awful; it was a rude awakening. *I'm still in the tunnel.* A man dressed in an EMT outfit sat holding her. He was handsome, but that was the last thing on her mind.

"Hey there, welcome back." His voice was low and fluid.

Her earbuds were no longer in.

She sat up abruptly. There were people everywhere. Before her was Earl's body. He was being photographed. The forensics team had arrived.

"Detective Bauer," she recognized this voice. It was her Captain.

"Captain," her head dropped low, ashamed, "I'm so sorry. I made some terrible calls."

"Oh, Bauer, if you only knew how wrong you are," his hair was silver from age and stress. He held a strong presence. "Can you walk?"

"I think so." She stood. Her legs felt weak, but walking was not impossible. The captain helped her stand and became her support. They locked arms, and he helped her as they walked together.

"We found Weber. He's alive, but barely. They are confident he will survive. Sadly, I cannot say the same for Crate. He died on the way to the hospital." He paused and brought her to the wall of entrails, Earl's *Starry Night*. "I'm sorry."

"It shouldn't have been that way."

"Don't do that to yourself. I know you will, but as your Captain, I'm telling you it is not your fault. This is the risk we all take coming to the job. I did, however, want you to see this." With a *click*, his light illuminated the art Earl made. *His masterpiece.*

Elizabeth gasped.

"This is what you stopped. Our earliest estimations are that he's likely been doing this for ten years or more, with God only knows how many victims. He got greedy and wanted to finish. Otherwise, who knows how long it would've taken to bust this guy."

Silence fell over the two.

"Take the pictures that you need for evidence, then destroy it," she whispered. "I don't want this leaking to the press. Earl wanted one thing and one thing only; fans to view his art." She paused and turned away. "We can't give that to him. You have to bury this."

"I agree," the Captain put his hand on Elizabeth. "Why don't you do your debriefing, then get out of here."

"Thanks, Captain." Elizabeth began to walk off, then stopped. "People like Earl are an evil that exists in this world. I just don't feel like the rest of the world needs to know that truth. Maybe I'm wrong, but I hope in my heart that even though I deal with evil daily, someone like me deals with the good every day, too. That's how I sleep at night."

THE ECLIPSE

No one believes me.

It was supposed to be the most amazing day of my life, but it became the most horrific nightmare. I should've listened to my mother when she warned me not to go alone. The doctors are telling me that I ingested some sort of hallucinogen. Someone slipped it to me. They say that what I saw was ridiculous and that there are no other confirming accounts. I don't know how that could be. Unless everyone else is either clued in or dead.

For posterity's sake, I decided to record what happened to me. If it is written down, no one can deny it, and if anything happens to me, my story will be known to the world, just like the popular videos on the Internet. I also want it to be known to the world that I have no plans, would never, and have never thought of committing suicide.

Please keep in mind that I had to change actual names in this story in order to keep identities hidden. Small details in this have been changed to protect me and hopefully not draw attention to myself. Everything else is a 100% factual retelling of the events.

It was the concert of the century. The *Deadly Violets* were doing an exclusive concert during the day. They were reportedly "vampires," so they only performed at night for outdoor concerts. What a fresh gimmick. Who would actually believe that, especially after it was done in a movie already? However, this was the eclipse. For one day, for roughly two and a half hours, a total lunar eclipse would stifle the sun and bring the night to the day. Normal lunar eclipses only lasted a few minutes, but this was scheduled to be the dead-center of the eclipse on Earth. This is how they would preserve their brand as Stoker's bloodsuckers.

It was a single-day event, but other acts took the stage earlier in the day, all leading to *The Deadly Violets*. My favorite style of music is Goth Industrial Electronic Metal, as I describe it to friends and family. I was lucky, or as it turns out, unlucky, to win the ticket lottery and get an exclusive pass. No one understood my obsession, but I hadn't a care in the world. I am a quiet reserved girl who just so happens a thirst for the night and everything it brings with it. This was my Charlie to the Wonka factory, my golden ticket to the biggest goth event in the world.

It was long and arduous travel to get out in the middle of a cleared-out section of the wilderness. Trees were freshly torn down, and a road crudely built of dirt just to arrive at the parking area. I chuckled as I drove out, thinking about climate change enthusiasts having meltdowns. Truth be told, there were probably a lot of environmentalists that would be at this concert enjoying themselves.

Parking was very easy, and I could already feel the buzz of energy from all the concert goers showing up. It was a surprisingly diverse group. There were girls wearing the Gogo boots and fur leggings, walking next to dudes in all black with radical hair in various points and colors. There was the hum of conversation with the occasional whoop and holler. It was a pack of ravenous dogs ready for a raucous day of pure music, energy, drugs, and all sorts of debauchery.

I was no stranger to that, and I was ready, eager, even.

Already, you could see the moon advancing on the sun. It appeared massive in the sky and felt otherworldly in the daytime. Standing there, I felt like I was in a sci-fi story. Seeing this lunar event surrounded by others who looked like aliens smelling the distinct mixture of alcohol, dust, body odor, and car exhaust. All of this culminated in an out-of-body experience like no other ,and excitement swelled up in me like a tidal wave forming on a beach. It was truly overwhelming.

Gigantic black towers were erected as the entrance to the venue.   Walkin g through, I noticed two large wooden doors pushed open to the side. It was like the entrance to Dracula's castle. I was home. For the first time in my life, I truly felt like I belonged. I just had no idea what nightmarish gore this new home had in store for me.

After what seemed like a decade of walking, my feet felt like anchors, and my sore legs ached for a breather. My spirit was stronger. That's when it came into view. The stage. This was real. My eyes widened as I tried desperately to soak it all in.

It was set on a slope shaped into a half-circle. There were absolutely no chairs; it was simply grass-sloping hills all leading down to the epicenter of a huge stage. This was like nothing I'd ever seen before. It was painted midnight black. Hanging around it and on the edge of the stage were more speakers than I had ever seen. This was going to be epic. It was a raised stage with a tiny gated fence that separated the fans from the stage only by a few feet, maybe just barely arm's length. I had to get to the front.

The bowl began to fill in with people, but I pushed and clawed my aching legs down to the front. I wasn't quite at the gate, but I was damn close. I stopped and claimed my space. I brought a water bladder to keep myself hydrated and a second of a similar colored liquid, but most definitely not water. I needed to be careful not to drink too much too fast. I would not be leaving this spot for the entirety of the concert, and I still had a few hours to go.

Time passed, and an early act came on to hype up the crowd and get them ready. I had never heard of them, but they weren't too bad. Their act was polished enough to hold a presence, but the field was still pretty sparse. Vendors lined the outside edges of the venue. I noticed a cute guy to my right. We locked eyes but still hadn't spoken a word. He had dark hair, broad shoulders, and nice arms. Could today be my day? I debated making the first move, but shyness overcame me. I was thankful that my long hair helped to hide my flush cheeks.

Again, we locked eyes as the darkness started to loom overhead. This is when I noticed that he had just the dreamiest green eyes. I thought to myself, *there is no way that I could be this lucky*. That's when I heard it.

"Hey, are you excited?"

I could barely hear him. The music was so loud.

"What?" I answered, and then it clicked what he said. I told him, "I'm super excited," and he repeated himself at the same time I answered. I felt stupid, but he giggled, so I giggled.

"Can I buy you a drink?" His voice was velvet and tickled me inside.

"Yes!"

"What would you like?"

"Anything with…" the music stopped. "…vodka!" Everyone around us heard me, and a large chuckle passed through the crowd.

"Hell yeah, let's all have some vodka," shouted the band's frontman, and another chuckle passed like a virus through the crowd.

I blushed.

He smiled. "I'll be right back."

The crowd cheered and clapped. I wasn't sure if I liked this attention or not.

The warmth of his smile reassured me and seemed to make everything better.

It felt like an hour had passed, and the opener left. It felt like dusk, but it was only two o'clock. The eclipse officially started at three. It was only another hour. A hype man was out asking if everyone was ready for *The Deadly Violets*. Others worked on sound check. We had one more opener to get through.

Suddenly, the Red Sea of concert-goers parted, and I saw him. Green eyes darting back and forth. Finally, he saw me, and a smile came across his face. There were four drinks in his hand. A couple guys reacted. Why hadn't I noticed he was with friends? I guess I was one of the weird ones who came by themselves. They grabbed their drinks, but he came over to me and handed a cocktail to me.

"Sorry that took forever," he shook his head and smiled.

I melted. "All good," I tried to play aloof. He was so cute.

"It was insanely expensive, and I had to sign over the rights to my liver." His face looked serious, and for a minute, I believed him. I don't know why. Then he cracked a smile and began to laugh.

I laughed, too, and for the first time, I could hear the ring of the amplifiers in my ears. It was a high-pitched buzz, not a natural one, but one born from an industrial gestation period as one adjusts to the decibels well above natural human tolerance.

"Thanks so much! I'm pretty sure you can survive without your liver, but you probably shouldn't drink." I laughed, he laughed, then I snorted like a fool.

To my chagrin, he didn't have a look of disgust at the swine that I had momentarily become. Instead, he looked at me endearingly. *Did he really think that was cute?*

"Don't you worry about me," his nice arms flexed as he gave me a thumbs up, and again I blushed. "I'm a vampire, so I'm pretty sure it will grow back, I think," he stammered, and his green eyes flashed at me again. "I'm pretty sure!"

I finally noticed that he was wearing a *Deadly Violets* shirt. I think he got it from the merch table. I could peek out another shirt sleeve just barely edging its way out, letting the world know of its existence. Below, he wore dark navy jeans that fit him quite well. To be honest, he had a cute butt, and for a second, I imagined him without them. I shook the thought out of my head, but a half smile materialized upon my face.

I felt like he was my perfect mate. My black fishnet sleeves, reached out below the *Deadly Violets* shirt I'd had for years. My short black cutoff shorts that frayed at the ends met with my nylon fishnet stockings, hugging and shaping my legs. They pressed my skin into hexagonal shape until they were hidden beneath my black industrial boots. I am a goth through and through, and anyone could size me up in a minute, but that was just fine. It was an image I enjoyed portraying, and obviously, it was working.

"Oh shit!" he said, shaking his head as his dark hair shook gently. "My name is Vincent, but my friends call me Vince," he immediately flew into nervous laughter. "I hate it."

"I like it. Nice to meet you, Vince. I am Rosaria."

At the front of the stage, the hype man walked back and forth. I wasn't really listening but suddenly picked up that he was now shouting about the eclipse. In a gruff voice, he shouted something like, 'We only have fifteen minutes until darkness falls. Then *The Deadly Violets* will emerge, and the bloodbath will begin!' He laughed a stupid villainous laugh. That needed some work.

With that said, he placed the mic back onto the stand and proceeded to exit stage left.

The next fifteen minutes felt like a dream. I hugged Vincent. We now stood embracing as the pre-recorded music blared through the PAs. Shadows grew until there were no shadows left to see. Lights emerged on the field and on the stage. It was brighter now than an hour ago, but now it was artificial light. I looked up at Vincent, lost in the moment. All reality and sense of time slipped away from me as I stared into those green eyes. This was happening so fast as we swayed to the music. In no time, we would be watching *The Deadly Violets* at their exclusive day concert, except now it was the darkest of days. I knew that I would never forget this.

That was for damn sure. There is no doubt that I will never forget any of this.

Finally, it was time for *The Deadly Violets*! The crowd erupted in applause, and a wave of energy surged through the crowd, seemingly reigniting the dead. I could see the singer in all her magnificence. The rest of the band members wake on stage in their dark Goth garments, and each donned their instruments.

At first, it was a slow melodic *boom boom* of the bass. Then the drums kicked in with a rapture snare to get things moving. Then came the distorted growl of the lead guitar. It was their newest single. Never before seen live. At least that's what I read in the forums on the Internet. The lead singer said it, too.

"We've never performed this live before. When I say *you*, I want you to say *death*."

Even her speaking was melodic, moody and majestic.

At this point, Vincent and I broke our bond and now stood cheering, jumping, and screaming as loud as we could.

By now, the eclipse was in full effect. It was as dark as the early hours of the morning. The lights went out on the crowd. The only people illuminated were the band itself. *The Deadly Violets* were on stage doing their thing. The screaming of the crowd grew to a fever pitch, and the melodic dark music cast a spell across the crowd. Spotlights filtered through the crowd, and for a second, I could've sworn that the number of people had doubled.

We all moved as one. A sea of people swaying back and forth. Songs seemed to come and go. Vincent and I would lock eyes and then return to moving with the crowd. It was pure and complete ecstasy. It was an experience I had never felt before, and I had been to too many music festivals at that point to keep count. The singer leaned over the stage between songs in all her beauty. She asked, 'How is everyone doing tonight?' It was amazing; like being born or breathing for the first time.

"This is amazing!" My hands reached for Vincent, but he was out of reach.

This suddenly pulled me from my fever dream. I looked around, but it was difficult to find him. I figured maybe he met with his boys for a second.

"Hello, all my dark darlings," the PA resounded across the stadium.

Everyone cheered, and all attention was cast on the stage. The crowd reacted in the same way. I was the odd one in the crowd, but no one noticed. I continued to look around for Vincent. There is no way I could go through all this and miss out on sharing it with him. I knew it was fate for me to meet him. I knew nothing of him except his name, yet I felt more connected to him than anyone I had ever met. Maybe blame it on the spell the music put me under, or maybe it was my desire getting the best of me. Either way, this feeling was a good thing.

"This is the time in our show," she moved to stage right and reached down to the dying fans. You could see people figuratively melt after touching her. "…the time where we feed. It's not easy being a vampire. I'm sure some of you can relate. We need blood to survive."

The crowd screamed, losing their minds.

Feed on me!

I'll be your sacrifice!

Choose me!

These were a few phrases I caught as people shouted, no begged, to be brought on stage with her. How could I blame them? She was gorgeous.

That's when I caught him… in my peripheral. It was Vincent. I picked out his dark hair, and the spotlight filled his face briefly. Was it his green eyes? Perhaps. They flashed at me.

My eyes adjusted to the dark, and I saw a look of ecstasy on his face as I realized another woman was there nuzzling on his neck.

My stomach hit like boulders being pushed off a cliff. I could almost hear it hit rock bottom and crash to the bottom of my bowel.

This isn't happening.

"Bring him out!"

An incredibly excited man was brought to the lead singer. He threw fist pumps into the air. I could tell this was the best day of his life. That was funny. My best day just turned into the worst day of my life. *Didn't Vincent and I have a connection? Why are boys this way?* I was devastated and completely pulled out of the spell they once had on me.

"My, you look tasty," she pointed the mic at him.

"Hell yah!" He brayed as his bald head hammered at the crowd. He threw out devil horns with his hands, and I could make out blurry tatted arms, but he was too far away to see any real detail. They were sleeves. That's all I knew, and he looked like he was a typical metalhead.

"Come here, darling."

Lights instantly turned red, including the lights that illuminated the field. It bathed everyone in a crimson blood shadow.

She embraced the man on stage, and his face went from euphoric to sudden panic. I could hear him shout in pain, and the mic quickly cut off.

For the first time since we arrived, all went silent. An uneasy sort of quiet without the sound of any living being. No crickets chirping, no birds singing, and not a single mouth blabbering. My stomach flipped, and I instantly began salivating like one does right before they vomit. Panic set in, and then flight kicked in. I wanted, no, I needed to leave. This was awful, and my whole body screamed from the inside out.

Heavy gain ripped as the frenetic distortion guitar rang out, cutting the silence in the most jarring way possible. I looked over at Vincent, heartbroken, terrified, and embarrassed that he had chosen someone else. I noticed his green eyes staring back at me, but something was wrong. They looked like glass eyes. Lifeless.

Then his head throttled back, exposing his torn, bloody neck. It was an open gash that looked like raw steak that had just been torn apart. My thoughts instantly went to a nature show I once watched about wolves. They showed their eating patterns and discussed how they hunted and attacked their prey's necks.

The woman singing on stage, who seemed so pretty just moments ago, now appeared hideous and terrifying. The bridge of her nose folded into gnarly, gnashing folds. Her brow was set so deep, and her eyes were an unearthly yellow color I had never seen before. Then I saw her teeth. My God, her teeth. Fangs protruded from the top of her mouth. My thoughts escaped elsewhere. I was at a haunted house. It's just a part of the show. Hollywood makeup and effects.

On stage, the man collapsed before her. No more devil horns. No life. The roadies began to drag the man off the stage. The lead singer now shouted something I didn't catch. I could only see crimson blood smeared around her lips and could only make out her terrifying fangs. The other band members playing their instruments also bared their fangs.

What she shouted must have been a war cry. Several people, or should I say monsters, appeared from behind the stage and jumped into the crowd. I don't know if I saw correctly, but their fingernails resembled claws. Their jumps were unearthly, and they seemed to glide gracefully as they did it.

Vampires.

They really were vampires. My gut screamed, and I should have listened, but I didn't. Instead, I tried to rationalize it. I didn't believe that this could actually be happening. There was no way.

I was not the only one going through this. I looked back at Vincent, and I saw that she had dropped him into a clump of a human knot. Bile escaped into my mouth. I coughed at the burn it created in my throat. Then I saw her. She was looking right at me. With a snarl, she pointed a clawed finger at me.

My, what big nails you have.

It was my mistake. I saw her for what she truly was. What was I supposed to do? I couldn't very well run. There were too many people. I backed up and ran into someone. Again, the music was rhythmic and humming loudly in my ears. Each step she made toward me was another burning riff on the guitar, a slam on the snare drum, and a mesmerizing slap on the bass.

I am going to die.

Warmth ran down my legs as my bladder gave way. I used to brag about having an iron bladder impervious to any music festival. Now, here I stood, urine running down my legs as I stared into the eyes of the devil. The devil who just killed my future, a man I could've had a future with, as she bared her ravenous teeth.

My, what big teeth you have.

There was nowhere to turn. Then I heard it. A shriek of an ungodly volume let loose through the crowd. The whole crowd erupted like an undersea volcano in the middle of the ocean. No one knew where the epicenter was, but madness broke out and turned into chaotic tidal waves of people folding over each other, hitting each other. Forcing each other out of the way and running as fast as possible to get out of the venue. There were screams, cussing, and so many guttural sounds it morphed into a new level of a language I wasn't fluent in, but I was speaking nonetheless.

As we all shouted in tongues, I turned and ran. I needed to get away from the person who killed my beloved. Get as far away from this concert as possible, but what was a 5'4" Goth girl to do in a sea of men and women raving madly, scrambling in the craziest dash for their lives possible? I turned and ran into a wall of human flesh. Instantly, I was knocked to my butt.

It hurt, but I shrugged it off.

I tried to rise again, but in no time, people tripped on me. I felt shoes collide with my sides. I felt my ribs crack like crab legs at a seafood restaurant. I smelled melted butter. That wasn't real. I just hugged my ribs, and more people fell upon me. I felt my skull crush against the ground.

All I remember now is seeing the spotlights searching through the crowd. The red light washed with the bright white lights as they moved across my face. The last image that ran through my head was the vision of the vampire who stole my love away from me. *Who were they?* Her pointy ears exacerbated her features.

My, what big ears you have.

There was a deafening blow to my head, and all went black. I don't remember anything after that.

****

Sunlight beckoned my closed eyes. It was blinding behind my eyelids. I could see the peach with red veins running deltas to the points in my eyes before I found consciousness. I felt delirious with a sense of dysphoria. My eyes closed with the night just to find myself lying below a sun-filled sky.

Finally, with unexpected effort, I opened my eyes to find a pile of bodies upon me. There were so many, and the weight came to me. It was hard to breathe as my chest compressed beneath them. Strangest of all, there was no sound. Just the sounds of nature. Birds chirping. Trees swaying to the wind. The hum of the world as if nothing had happened at all.

Until the sirens quickly interrupted the quiet.

I couldn't breathe. I tried to shout, but nothing escaped my throat. I tried desperately again. Still nothing.

They were close. I could see red and blue cascading off the fixtures from the concert.

I tried to push my way out, but the weight of the bodies was too much. I could barely breathe, let alone scoot out. I had survived, but what kind of survival was this?

"This is the police. Is there anyone out there?"

I could hear it. I didn't know what to do besides lay there desperately trying to shout.

Footsteps crunched around me. It felt as if they were right behind me. I squirmed even harder, but still, it felt like it came to no avail.

Could this be the end?

The steps faded away.

Will I aspirate, and they'll find my corpse just to collect it with the others?

I felt dripping on my forehead, and the claustrophobia gave me enough energy to fight.

With one final push, I shouted.

"Aaaghhh!"

Silence in response.

"We have a live one!" someone shouted.

Boots crunched and approached my way. I was saved. I would be pulled from this nightmare. I'd wake up soon to my normal life filled with light and no darkness.

Again, I felt my existence fading. That was all I had left. As I faded, I felt strong hands beneath me. With a dragging motion that made me feel as though I was floating, I receded from below the pile of bodies with one fell swoop. I was out.

Then, I was mentally out.

****

The next thing I knew, my blurry eyes opened slowly as I observed a plain white room. There was a television as well as medical instruments. I knew exactly where I was. It was a hospital. The smell of chemicals, the dry taste making my mouth feel like sandpaper, and the bland everything. It was so bright, but I couldn't complain.

I looked around, still in a daze. My head pounded and ached. I was confused. I couldn't remember anything of how I got there. No car ride, reason, or possible explanation for why I suddenly woke up in a hospital.

"Hi there, Rosaria. I'm glad you're back with us. This is a good day."

All I could see was a white lab coat and a dark-skinned man shining a light in my eyes. The first few hours were extremely fuzzy. I remember him asking questions. I remember him asking several of the same questions, but I don't remember answering them the same way.

I was told that I was found at the concert. I was found unconscious; there seemed to be an issue with the water supply.

I listened but could say nothing. Honestly, I couldn't protest as there was nothing I could protest about. I couldn't remember a thing.

Then all of that changed.

****

I sit now before you. I have all the memories. I did not drink any bad water. There was nothing like that there. To Vincent's parent's I'm sorry I couldn't have done more. I didn't expect any of it.

The Deadly Violets being vampires was supposed to be a gimmick. It wasn't supposed to be anything serious. It was for show, but obviously, that was not true. The eclipse was everything they needed. It was all the excuse they needed to come out in the daylight. For all of them to feed.

Do not go to a *Deadly Violets* concert.

They are exactly what they say. The Eclipse was a mistake. I should have never gone. I don't even know why I did. It was supposed to be the absolute best day of my life. Instead, it turned into my biggest nightmare.

Now, no one believes me. Will you? I write this in posterity. If anything should happen to me. Remember that I would never kill myself or do anything of the sort!

Will you believe me?

I WILL ALWAYS HAVE MY FANS

This is a terrible story.

The analog clock ticked incessantly in the waiting room. Curtis' hands were sweaty as he waited with bated breath. This was the most important meeting of his life. This was it. Everything hinged on it. He spent over a year writing this book. It was his magnum opus. Today, he was meeting with a publisher. Up until this point, no one believed in his ability to write. Not his family, his girlfriend (ex-girlfriend), not even his friends who were supposed to be by his side. No one.

That's okay; he would show them.

He had already met with two other publishers who rejected it. They offered feedback, but Curtis knew the rejection came because this meeting was the important one. This particular New York publisher had published his hero's work before him. The stuff of nightmares, fiction that wouldn't let you sleep. Those authors paved the way for people like Curtis.

An orchestral version of *Hotel California* was playing in the lobby. He thought it interesting as a lyric popped into his head, "You can check out anytime you like, but you can never leave."

"Curtis?"

Oh, that's me! This is my time to shine. My dream will come true today.

****

"This is a terrible story."

Jutting up his head with a puzzled look, Curtis thought he had heard incorrectly.

"I'm sorry, did you just say…" as he placed both hands on the desk in front of him, they began to tremble.

"No, *I'm* sorry." The man's lips twisted into a snarl, causing mustache hairs to stand on end. "I'm sorry I had to read this."

The printed manuscript was tossed across the table with little regard. Unstapled, the papers slid in disjointed unity like a pile of trash blowing in the wind. *Trash.* Curtis sat devastated and confused. His dream now lay scattered about the table; tossed at him with such apathetic praise.

"I don't understand. You said you liked the concept." Curtis fumbled with the papers, trying to put them back into a neat pile. Maybe if he did this, then his life, too, would be back in order.

"Look, the concept was good. It just takes too long to get going." The man stroked his bushy mustache as he spoke. He held an air of arrogance, sitting upright. "Modern readers need action right away. If you don't hook them in the first few words, then you lose them forever."

"Sir, I can re-write this. I can get the action going. It's a horror story, sir. What about the ambiance?" Curtis desperately tried to keep this option open. He didn't want to lose an opportunity.

It was too late. The burly executive had already walked to the door and held it open. It was a polite way to say, '*You need to leave now.'*

Curtis stood clumsily as the manuscript fell out of his hands. *How fitting.* This was his world right now, scattered haphazardly upon the floor. It was a terrible story.

"Listen, kid."

Kid? thought Curtis. *We're close to the same age. At least, I think we are.*

"Leave ambiance to those who already have faithful readers. It's a different audience."

It was the first time Curtis heard empathy in his hoarse voice. However, when Curtis looked at him, the man's face portrayed impatience as he waited. *So much for empathy.*

Finally, gathering his life in his hands, Curtis walked out. Before he could turn in one last ditch effort to keep the door open, the man had already let the door go, and it swung with a deafening *click*, just inches away from hitting him on his way out.

Defeated and head hanging low, Curtis approached the reception desk, unable to make eye contact with the receptionist. He put his parking ticket on the desk in front of him.

"Um, we don't validate parking." The receptionist pushed the ticket back with a flamboyant air.

"Oh," was the only sound that escaped Curtis' mouth. *Of course, you don't validate parking.*

"How'd it go in there?" The receptionist asked.

For the first time, Curtis looks up and noticed the multi-colored short hair on the man. He wore one silver dangling earring of a Celtic cross and appeared to be wearing blush.

"Yeah, you know, okay. I've got some notes and things to correct before taking the next step." *Lies. All lies.* It's hard to tell the truth when you feel like a failure. When your dreams are tossed about like useless letter print in 8.5" x 11" pages filled with rambling gobble-di-goop. *Ambiance.*

Action? Where is the action?

"Great. I always feel like I'm about to meet the next Stephen King or H.P. Lovecraft, you know?" He smiled with cherry-red lips.

Curtis mumbled in place of an actual answer. *If only. That guy didn't know anything about horror. How it's better as a slow burn. It's not all jump scares and grotesque kills. It's the ambiance that gets you.*

Curtis boarded the steel elevator. It smelled musty and stale. Pressing the B5 button, it went into the depths of publisher hell. It was the walk of shame and descent of a failing author. *Time to grab my shitty story and hop in my shitty car for a shitty drive home.*

It may have been his imagination, or it may have been his crushed heart, but it seemed to get colder as he descended to the parking garage located under the building. An involuntary shiver came over him as he broke out into goose-pimples. With a *ding*, suddenly, the steel doors opened to the underground garage, awakening him from his daze of self-pity.

Still, he held onto his manuscript, pinning it between his arms as a gush of wind ran past him when the doors opened. The wind ruffled the papers. Another reminder of his "masterpiece" and how it had fallen from his once proud hold on it.

He stepped out into the cold, dry parking garage immersed in grey with a hint of scarred yellow paint, that seemed to cry: "Yield, please do not scrape against my concrete interior!" The gush of wind was probably caused by the change in air pressure. Everything was now still. Not a sound. His footsteps echoed loudly as he stepped out of the elevator. A fluorescent light flickered in the distance. It was eerie, to say the least.

"Ambiance!" he said aloud to himself. "*This* is ambiance. Now, *this* is a setting for a horror story." He imagined himself back in that executive's office. In his mind's eye, he was defending himself.

****

"Ambiance is where it's at. The audience needs to be in the mood; otherwise, how can a scare affect them?" He walked in a proud gate juxtaposing his imposter syndrome. "The answer to horror is ambiance. It's what sets it apart from any other literary style."

"Ah! I see now. I just hadn't been able to understand your story. My vision was far too narrow, and I did not give any respect to the audience," the imaginary whiskered executive stated. "A book deal is in store for you. What do you say, a hundred thousand?"

"Oh my! That sounds good, but I was hoping for a two hundred thousand deal with a contract for a second book," imaginary Curtis stated proudly, standing over the groveling executive.

"You've got it!" came the reply, and Curtis smiled.

****

Suddenly, a loud banging echoed through the parking garage. Curtis was startled. He looked around for the source, but it was indiscernible. The echoes made it too difficult. He was instantly pulled from his daydream. He stopped and stood still for a second, trying to listen. The space was unusually loud.

Realizing he wasn't breathing, Curtis exhaled and sucked in the stale air. Then, once the feeling subsided, he chuckled at himself.

"See. The ambiance gives way to the creepy feeling, making random noises scary," he laughed aloud as he spoke to himself. "Now, *this* would make a great scene for a horror movie." Already, the wheels in his head began to turn as he thought about how to write the scene.

Ding!

The elevator doors opened. Curtis looked back, but no one was there.

His heart began to beat a little faster. *Thump, thump, thump! Why did the elevator just open?* He couldn't see directly into it, but it didn't seem to hold anyone. Just standing there, he watched in bated anticipation for what came next. With another *ding,* the doors started to close when suddenly a hand from the ether stopped them.

A pretty woman with blonde hair and long legs emerged from the elevator. She was on her cell phone, and her other hand carried a black leather bag. She was dressed professionally with an air of legality to her. *A lawyer? Perhaps.* She glided out on her heels, asking into her phone if the person could hear her.

"Damn it," she whispered to herself. Looking up, she saw Curtis staring.

"Can I help you?" she asked while jabbing at the phone with her finger in annoyance.

"Sorry." Curtis forgot he was staring. Authors are odd folk. Always watching, sometimes with ignorance, that others can see them. It was easy to forget that they weren't the narrator from their stories. The stories where they played God. Where they could casually observe people acting out their lives. Never to be seen or attested.

Click, click went her heels in a rhythmic tone that sounded so familiar to Curtis. *What was that song?* He could hear her mumble something to herself about the homeless. *Do I really look that hopeless?*

"Seriously, mind your own business," she shoved the phone back into her purse, annoyed and frustrated.

He turned in shame, intending to walk back to his car, wherever he parked. This place seemed so much larger than when he initially parked. He was certain he was on the right level and tried to recall if he walked in the right direction. It didn't seem to take this long to get to the elevator. Maybe he passed the car while distracted in his daydream, but he didn't want to look back. He didn't want to cause any more issues with this lady. She was already a walking reminder of his loneliness. It's not like he had anyone at home to help him lick his wounds. His girlfriend of a few years walked out on him months ago because she said he wasn't ambitious enough.

Twerp, twerp went a car keeping in rhythm with her heel clicks. Curtis dared not look again but waited for the sound of a door opening, which seemed to take longer than he expected.

Aaaghhh!

It was a blood-curdling cry, and it echoed so loud that it hurt Curtis' ears. He looked toward the lady who just sassed him but couldn't see her behind the row of cars. His legs wanted to move, wanted to help, but he didn't know where to go. *Where is the sound coming from?* The chamber of echoes made it nearly impossible to track.

The cry continued until Curtis heard a wet crunch, and just like that, the screaming stopped. Curtis had never heard anything like that in his life. He stood, frozen.

Move, damn it!

Finally, his legs complied, and he ran to where he last saw her, weaving between two cars parked annoyingly close together. He finally reached the end, but she was not there. Looking around frantically, he didn't know where to look next. Then he stopped, took a breath, and visualized the sound the car made just seconds ago. That's when he remembered. *It should be to the right of where I'm standing.*

Turning, he saw a trail of red. *Blood!*

His hand jutted to his mouth as he gasped. Part of him urged him to leave. *Get out now!* But the bigger part of him wouldn't allow it. *What if she is badly hurt?*

Ignoring his instinct, he followed the trail. It looked like someone had spilled marinara sauce as they were running. The pool was large and shallow. It led to the end of a vehicle, and he followed the trail to her face, lying on the ground. He saw her blank eyes and mouth agape as she was dragged off out of view behind another vehicle.

Curtis froze again, questioning reality. *There is no way this is really happening.* It was something straight out of one of his own stories. Something that didn't happen to normal folk.

"Miss, are you okay?" Curtis cupped his hands to his mouth as if that would make any difference.

Silence. No answer.

Curtis walked forward despite his intuition telling him not to. He still clutched the manuscript in one hand and in the other hand, his car keys. Following the blood trail, he slowly approached where he had last seen her. A moment's hesitation, and he turned to look behind the car.   He was not prepared for what he saw next.

A dismembered hand was surrounded by a sea of scarlet. It looked like a spilled platter of spaghetti, but instead of noodles, it was an arm. The smell of iron, the unmistakable smell of blood, wiped the image of spaghetti from his mind.

Quickly, he turned away. He tried to choke down vomit and ignored everything in his body, screaming at him to faint. He turned back to look again, though not sure why. He witnessed a small, gray-clawed hand grab the dismembered limb and drag it underneath the nearby car. The movement was immediately followed by another wet crunch.

Bone crunched and flesh ripped. His mind tried to replace these sounds with endearing thoughts. The crunch of a cracker when he was sick. The sound of biting into a piece of pork. Anything to justify the reality before him.

Panic set in. He turned away. The woman was dead; he was sure of that. *What did I just see?* Even he didn't understand. *This isn't really happening. It has to be a dream.* He was desperate to cling to normalcy. *Don't stray into the supernatural. Keep yourself grounded.*

How do I get out of here? Where do I go? If only I'd paid attention to where I parked the car. There were two exits now. His vehicle or the elevator.

He shook his head. The elevator was a bad idea. Pressing the button, awaiting its arrival, and then waiting for the doors to close. That's way too much time to allow himself to be attacked. Now, he could try to get to his car, but without knowing exactly where it was, this also left him open to attack. He could press the lock button on his keyfob, but that would honk the horn, alerting the attackers where to go. *What do I do?*

Crunch, crunch, crunch.

Oh God, I can hear her bones being snapped. Slowly, he stepped around the car where he was hiding. He would carefully try to find his car, and if he had to, he would run like a child. *That's all I can do.*

He took each step intentionally. Slow, easy, with little to no noise. His eyes wandered left, then right, scanning each car, trying to find the identifying marks of his own vehicle. He could hear a loud ruckus from where he stood moments ago.

He could not find his vehicle. He couldn't handle the pressure. Curtis beeped the keyfob. Still another twenty feet ahead, he watched the brake lights flash. It was like heaven communicating with him. First, his feet, then the rest of his body complied. Fully committed, he ran.

Fifteen feet.

Ten feet.

Five feet.

Suddenly, he saw several small men. No, small brutes now appeared before his vehicle. They approached in a group. Their mouths were large and filled with sharp teeth. There was hair scattered about their face and head. In fact, their heads seemed to encompass at least fifty percent of their bodies. *What are these things?* They were particularly savage. Their small arms were equipped with large, clawed hands. Their small bodies allowed them to hide behind vehicles and maneuver in small areas. Their little legs were stout but muscular. They numbered at least ten, maybe more, but Curtis didn't have the time to count.

They chittered back and forth between them. *Gibberish?* No. This was a different language. One he was not familiar with but one that was natural to the group. *What the hell is that?* It was obviously communication, and it was terrifying.

"What are you?" Curtis tried to turn, but more were behind him. He was definitely outnumbered. Twenty or more scary little men now surrounded him.

"It's not your business. We are your nightmares. We are what you dream up when you are desperate and alone. We do not exist. We are eaters of humans. We do not judge. We do not care." *Is this one the leader? It is rather well-spoken despite their savage appearance.*

Little tufts of hair peaked out from cracks and wrinkles from its slab-colored skin. Besides its concrete appearance, the creature had a mouth of amazingly sharp teeth. The pupils were red, which made him think of the blood that surrounded the woman's arm. On the edges of its teeth, the blood-stained, like the tarter that even the best toothpaste couldn't remove. Each step rapped on the concrete floor, like a plastic cone being dropped in a construction zone. Curtis could have easily confused the creature with the concrete floor or other construction paraphernalia in the area, if it hadn't spoken.

As it approached, he smelled the musty stench of skunk. It smelled similar to a road kill. However, this was much more overpowering, as if the skunk had just sprayed without warning. He suddenly remembered a trip to the zoo when he was a child, but this was no zoo. There were no guard rails. No gates. Nothing barring him from the exhibits. He melted against the concrete post.

"Please! Please don't kill me!"

Suddenly, the well-spoken creature lunged forward, teeth gnashing in snarled fierceness.

Curtis staggered to his feet and stumbled clumsily backward, falling again. With a slam, his head smacked the concrete, and his gray universe became blurry. His manuscript was splayed across his chest and the floor. *This is it. This is the end.*

With the small pressure of a young child, Curtis could feel the creature's weight upon him. It crawled up on his chest. Slowly, it raised its clawed hand high up into the air. Awaiting

the gift of midnight, Curtis accepted the sweet darkness that
followed one's death. There were no flashbacks of his
childhood like people claimed, just the weight of anxious dread
waiting for the pain of dagger-like claws. To his surprise, after
closing his eyes to prepare for the blow, he felt… nothing.

Instead, there was the lightest pressure on his chest. It
almost tickled. Curtis opened one eye to see what was
happening. His other eye opened, and together they grew wide.
Instead of being dismembered and eaten, this creature held up
a page of his manuscript. It appeared to be reading. His jaw
dropped as he tried to understand the scene.

The other creatures slowly walked forward, closing the
circle around him. After a few seconds, the creature looked at
the others. He grunted something guttural that Curtis didn't
quite understand. Suddenly, the others began to pick up the
pages of his manuscript.

"What the hell?" Curtis shifted onto his elbows. *How
hard did I hit my head on that concrete? Is this really happening?* There
was no shortage of questions.

"More…" said the creature with a graveled voice, still
holding that page of the manuscript directly before its
primordial eyes.

Then he felt it. The little creature stepped off of his
abdomen. The weight seemed to lift, and for a second, he could
have sworn he was floating.

*Am I already dead? This is ridiculous, but is it? Maybe this is
my hell.*

"Bring us more stories." Each creature held scattered
pages from his manuscript in their claws.

They slowly walked back, and he watched as they vanished into the concrete environment around him.

Something spoke to Curtis. The voice told him this was not a request. It was a threat. Images of the gore of that poor woman strewn apart in pieces flashed before his eyes. The sound of the wet crunch resonated in his ears. An involuntary shudder passed through his whole body. Terror sank in once again, only to be instantly relieved with the twitch of his hand.

That was real. He sat up. The lead creature, who had done all the talking, repeated its demand.

"Bring us more stories."

"I… I will," Curtis managed, his voice crackling. "I promise."

Curtis was alive, somehow saved by his story. The irony of the situation did not elude him. *This was a terrible story.* Yet somehow, his terrible story had just extended his life. Curtis meant what he said by the promise. A light of unfinished business was lit inside him. It was a second chance, a new seal on life that, once broken, needed fulfillment. His fingers ached for the keyboard. His soul longed to create. His bowels ached with the nerves of a near-death experience. This was his time. He would be back. He would bring them more stories.

****

This is a great story!

Jutting up his head, puzzled, Curtis thought he had heard incorrectly.

"I'm sorry, did you just say…" He placed both hands on the desk in front of him. They began to tremble.

"Don't be sorry, kid." *There's that phrasing again. Am I dense?* Curtis was sure they were closer in age. Again, the man's mustache hair furled as he stated, "I'm sorry. I didn't think you had what it takes."

"Well, I guess you can say I was inspired after our last meeting." The trembling stopped. Curtis now sat with a new air of arrogance and confidence. It is a good mixture for a writer.

"I love it!" The large man stood at his desk, hand extended, awaiting the professional handshake. Curtis complied. "We will get to work right away. There are steps we need to follow, but getting you the best publishing deal is our priority."

"Thank you, sir. I'm very interested in seeing what you come up with. I have others interested as well." Curtis turned to the door with confidence. This time, he'd open the door and wouldn't let it hit him on the way out.

"Well, let's just wait one minute," the large man tried to stop him by placing a hand on his shoulder. "I can guarantee we have the best deals."

"Then let me know when you have one." With a smile, Curtis turned and left, his manuscript still in hand. He held his head high and left with confidence.

The door shut behind him, but it didn't seem to slam or startle him. Instead, it was a nice, respectful usher out. The receptionist, in all his flamboyant fashion, looked at him.

"How'd it go this time?"

"Great. I'm sure he'll get back to me with a deal in no time."

"I knew you were one of the greats." A smile flashed across his nicely manicured face. "I just knew. Now, let me validate your parking."

Curtis laughed. *Of course.*

Curtis could've left and never returned, but why would he do that? He found his readers. Maybe the publisher didn't like his story. Fine. He could deal with that, but there was something much more important than that before him. For the first time, he had readers. He had always wanted to be involved with this publisher, and he'd do anything. He'd sell his soul if he had to. These creatures had taught him a good lesson.

They wanted him to live, to continue on to make the stories that they loved. The leader read his work and could communicate with the rest of the brood. This is why Curtis came back. Any sane man would've left and never come back. Not Curtis. Not this time. For the first time in his life, he wasn't running away.

DING! The elevator opened. The descent was familiar but had a different twist. This was the story. The story he had waited for. The one that made the difference. It started with a bang. The action. The ambiance was built in. A story for modern audiences. This was it.

With another *ding* he was presented with the familiar concrete under the corporate jungle. This time, he had a smile on his face. No sign of fear. As he walked out, he saw the half-tubular-like pillars before he walked to the parking area. He almost passed it but stopped. Slowly, he placed the manuscript in his hand atop the pillar. Looking down, he smiled once again before continuing to his vehicle.

"Thank you," a gravely voice echoed through the garage floor. "More…"

Without turning to look back, Curtis smiled.

"There will be plenty more. I will always have my fans."

THE OLD LADY WHO SOLD ROSES

Wind swept the sand, making another dusty crimson sunset upon the marketplace. It was a place of historic relevance, for it had not been touched by progress or human advances. Located down an old clay-baked brick street it was a bazaar where anyone could get their necessities as well as some extravagance. During the day, it was the main center for commerce in this backward foreign town. People swarmed to get their meals, their clothing, or jewelry. Each day was busy and thankless for a vendor. However, this bazaar had become known for its perfect, beautiful red roses.

At dusk, the bazaar did not resemble its gloriousness of the mid-day rush. Instead, it was a lonely street with the only ones left being the vendors. Each night, the vendors would go through their products and either throw away or give away their bad products. That is, all except one vendor, the old lady who sold roses. Each day she sold out completely.

No one knew how long she had been selling there, but they all despised her. Each day she came, she would clip her perfect red roses and sell every last one before nightfall. Most days, she left while it was still the afternoon. Each morning, they came, and a line had already formed at her stand. The line never dwindled until she ran out each day. All the while, the other vendors sneered and gnashed their teeth at her prosperity. They knew her name but preferred to call her The Old Lady Who Sold Roses.

Despite the fact that they knew her name, not much was known about her personal life. No one knew whether she had a family, for no one ever came with her. Her movements were slow, and her body shook with each step. Walking to her stand, she always had a shawl covering her head, hiding her stringy grey and white hair. Deep wrinkles contoured the many features of her face. Brown eyes were sunken into her head, and a burgundy-peach ring outlined them under her brow. Peeking out from under the shawl was her wart-covered nose, which almost decisively gave her a frightful appearance. This, coupled with her soft yet shrill voice that escaped a toothless mouth save for a few, accentuated it.

Children steered clear of The Old Lady With The Roses, and rumors of witchcraft and spells buzzed about the market. Each time kids came and played near her stand, she would quickly shew them away like they were mice in a pub. Once, a customer who grew impatient in the line mishandled one of her rose bushes and received a small cut from a thorn. She became furious and told him never to come back. This man ended up sick for weeks. No doctor in the area could explain it. For years, the other vendors spoke to each other in whispers that something must be done about her.

No one dared to try.

Every morning, she seemed to perform a ritual and then a different one at the end of every day. Vendors would watch as she arrived each morning. Meticulously, she entered her stand, which had twelve rose bushes in pots on shelves behind the table and three larger bushes on the table itself. Each bush yielded perfect budding roses of an ideal length. Each morning, she cajoled her rose bushes, showering them with compliments and touching them tenderly yet methodically. That is when she pruned the roses carefully, making each cut. Her skill level was unmatched, and she worked quickly and carefully, never cutting herself or damaging her bushes.

At the end of every day, she would close her shop, selling every rose, and once more tended to her bushes. During this time, she would sing songs in a strange language, carefully caressing each branch and new bud. Never once cutting herself, she ran her fingers over each thorny branch and twig. No one could distinguish which language she sang, for she sang in a low voice, nearly a whisper. Finally, she would water each bush at the end of each song and return them to their respective places. Once she was done with her ritual, she bid each one good night and then asked each bush to provide beautiful roses for her tomorrow.

Every new day was a repeat of the last. She arrived, and every rose bush had fulfilled her request, bearing the most perfect roses for their caretaker.

This day was no different than any other. The morning rush came and went. Each vendor was busy. Clothing fared well, jewelry sold slowly, produce had a regular rush at lunch and just before dinner, and the meats had a similar turnout. Yet once again, The Woman Who Sold Roses had completely sold out of her flowers. It was a later day than normal for her, and she began her nightly ritual as the last few shoppers made their final purchases and then cleared out of the Bazaar.

Winds had turned direction suddenly, and a madness seemed to be swept in with it. Each vendor began to go through their product and trash the non-sellers or spoiled pieces. It began as a mumble by each one, frustrated at the thought of never selling out. Vendors whose stands were close together began to talk in frustration about how they never seemed to sell enough. Darkness began to creep over the bazaar as the sun set in its ordinary fashion. The complaining and mumbling of the venders increasingly became a dull roar. That was, until the old woman's singing was carried with the wind and interrupted them all.

"Codladh anois mo lomhara. Alainn ta sin a eile, fanacht an ag ardu ghrian," the song was soft and gentle. It came off as mystical and eerie to those ears who received the words.

It was a tongue that was unknown and not recognized by the vendors. This incantation interrupted their squabbling, and they all turned to glare at the old lady. Now, the vendors came together, for they had found a new source for all their problems. They stood in the center of the market and talked in hushed tones.

"How is it that she sells all her roses every day, and I'm stuck here throwing away half of my product every day!" the big man who sold produce stated angrily.

"Why, just today, I sold three of my gold necklaces for less than I paid for them. Just to get rid of them," complained the irritable woman who sold jewelry. "Yet there isn't a single rose left, not even those with a blemishes!"

"When I came in today, I found that a rat had eaten through an entire pile of my shirts!" the woman who sold fashionable clothing hoarsely whispered in anger. "Though no bugs, birds, or other pests ever eat her roses!"

"Each night, I spend hours trying to fix my furniture with loose legs because people don't think that they are quality. Yet every night, I watch as she leaves her stand before anyone else!" grumbled the short, stocky furniture salesman.

"I spend countless hours trying to acquire decent antiques to sell people," hissed the old man wearing specs. "Then, she shows up to perfectly budded rose bushes every morning! She doesn't spend any time pruning the flowers she sells that day!"

With each passing statement, anger and frustration began to boil over. Suddenly, someone from the group threw the word 'witchcraft' into the mix. It was hard to tell who said it since everyone was talking at once. However, it did the trick, and suddenly the conversation turned. Fear was now introduced, and the conversation began to grow louder. Still, The Old Lady Who Sold Roses continued to perform her ritual, seemingly oblivious to the group.

"It all makes sense," said the potter who had remained largely quiet. "Every morning and every evening, she talks to her roses. She *caresses* her roses. She *sings* to her roses. Then, every day, she has *perfect* roses!" He grew increasingly more agitated with each sentence, and he looked back to his stand which was filled with pottery. Two pots were stacked there with cracks waiting to be thrown away.

"We can't forget about the man that she cursed!" started the jeweler. She sneered as she continued. "All he did was gently touch her rose bush, and she yelled curses at him. He was sick for weeks. I heard from his wife that he is a lame husband. He used to work and make a living, and now, since his sickness, he just sits around despite being healthy!"

"Something needs to be done!" shouted the big man who sold produce. "I will not stand for having a witch at our market!"

The wind blew hard now. It was this same wind that blew in the madness. As it blew harder, the madness grew, which now began to turn violent. Fear always leads to hate, as madness leads to violence, so when there is a combination of both, tragedy is bound to prevail. Just an hour ago, the vendors were cordial and pleasant, selling their merchandise to customers. Now, they were a dark reflection of themselves, gnashing teeth and plotting murderous thoughts.

"She needs to go!" someone shouted from the crowd. It couldn't be determined who it was, but it caught on, and several others cheered.

"Wait." the short, stocky furniture salesman raised his hand and quieted his voice. "What if she curses all of us for driving her out?"

"Who's to say that she hasn't already cursed us with having to rid ourselves daily of bad product?" the potter interjected.

"Then I suppose we will just have to get rid of her in another way," suggested the spectacle-wearing antiques dealer.

"What are you suggesting?" asked the jeweler.

"I think we all know what we have to do," the big produce seller stated loudly, inciting the mob. A darkness grew across his brow, and a deranged smile spread across his face.

The wind kicked up dust, blowing even harder now, and the whole market seemed to be shaking violently from the wind. The old lady, still so enraptured with her ritual of singing and dressing her roses, did not notice. If she had looked up, she would have seen the large crowd approaching her. It was hard to tell through the dust, but their faces were deranged, murderous, even. It was as if they had an appetite for violence and they were starving.

In front of her was her last rose bush, and she gently ran her hands along each branch, singing to it. Malevolently, the mob walked toward her. Their hands shook with rage, and their feet stomped with anger. Tempers rose, and madness set in. Tonight, a tragedy would take place, and the wind whistled with intent to destroy. This peaceful bazaar, buzzing with life, had become a nightmare brooding death.

What ensued next was total chaos. Finally, the old woman heard the group and looked up. She let out a scream as she realized that it was too late to run. The group came down on her together. Some hands choked, others punched, legs kicked and stomped. A frenzy had unleashed on the poor old lady who could not defend herself. Every member of the group contributed to the murdering chaos.

It was no time before the deed was done. However, this still didn't satisfy their madness. There was a lust for more. Someone shouted, "Destroy the roses!" With madness such as it was, the people overlooked their wounds as they all grabbed a rose bush and tore it apart with their hands. These people turned savage, and blood was drawn as the thorns of the bushes desperately tried to defend themselves. The vendors viciously ripped at the bushes as the bushes ripped at the vendor's hands.

Finally, it was over. The wind died down, and the rage subsided. Looking around, the vendors seemed confused yet satisfied with what was done. Upon the ground laid the estranged body that once held the old lady's life inside it. Now, it was a crumpled heap, surrounded by pieces of her famous rose bushes scattered about her. They formed a frame that encircled her. Each pot, was now topsy-turvy on its side, some were smashed and others completely upside down.

Each vendor looked down at their hands in fright and disgust. They were bloody and torn up from the thorns of the bushes. Glancing back and forth from their hands to the devastation before them, it was as if they couldn't fathom that they were responsible for all of this. They managed to destroy a place that sold beauty and love through their selfish hatred and fear. Many wondered what was next.

"What have we done?" piped up the jeweler, afraid of the consequences.

"It's fine," the big produce man said. "When she is found tomorrow, we will say we all left before her."

Everyone seemed to agree, although their faces were wrought with guilt. Suddenly, the big man who sold produce began to cough. It got violently worse, and quickly, he was brought to his knees and then to all fours. His back arched violently, and blood spewed from his mouth. Within seconds, he keeled over and was stone-dead on the ground. Others gasped and shrieked in fear. Murmurs went through the crowd, and someone whispered frantially, "The curse!"

Suddenly, everyone began to cough. Now, the murderous bunch emulated the produce vendor and were on their hands and knees. Blood came out of their mouths, and one by one, every single one of them keeled over stone-dead on the ground. It truly had become a sight to be seen as The Old Lady With The Roses lay in a crumpled heap surrounded by her torn-apart roses. Beside her, those who were responsible for her death all lay on the ground in a clumped group less magnificently splayed on the dirt.

Madness had come and gone with the passing wind. All that remained was death. Blackness fell over the Bazaar as night devoured the light. Menace could still be felt in the air as the coolness of the night settled over the land. Destruction never seemed so poetic as the justice of the roses. What happened next was ever more mysterious.

Dawn broke with the sun's redness, peering over the horizon and casting light upon the ravaged rose stand. It wasn't long before the usual partisans flooded the bazaar to line up for the roses. Though they came for beauty, all they discovered was horror and macabre. Mothers covered their children's eyes, and screams of surprise and panic escaped their mouths. Even men cast aside their eyes from what they saw. Local authorities were ushered in.

No authority had ever seen anything quite like the scene unfolding in front of them. The rose stand was in shambles, with smashed pots and scattered bodies. However, that was not the unusual part. The Old Lady Who Sold The Roses lay in the center of the stand, and scattered in a circle around her lifeless body were the pieces of the rose bushes. Each rose had bloomed overnight. As the police soaked in the crime scene before them, they saw a ring of beautiful, perfect roses enshrouding their caretaker as if they were grieving her passing. In an odd way, it was beautiful.

Below the circle of roses were the other vendors curled into odd shapes on the ground grotesquely. The stench of death could not be covered by the sweet scent of the fallen roses. It was fairly easy for the authorities to determine how the old lady came to her demise; however, it became a great mystery what had happened to the murderous vendors. They searched the area in earnest, trying to discover the solution to the question. Several people whispered 'witchcraft' under their breath.

However, the lead authority could not, with a good constitution, accept this as the reason. It was his job to be analytical and use logic for his findings. He took in the scene and began to search for possible clues. It wasn't long before he found a large jar under the front part of the rose stand. As he analyzed it, he could see that it was a brown-colored glass with a handle tapered slowly to the top. On top, a cork was stuck into the bottle.

It made a popping sound as he removed the cork. He sniffed the bottom of the cork. It was a familiar smell. Although he couldn't quite put his finger on it, he tried to link his memory to the aroma. Kneeling down, he picked up one of the broken rose pieces and sniffed the stem. He discovered the same pungentscent . It was much lighter, but it was unmistakable. Once again, the aroma flooded his senses, and his memory ran rampant, trying to determine the source. He determined already that the vendors had killed this old woman and had ripped the rose bushes to pieces. Their hands had several pre-mortem cuts and tears.

Still, their cuts were odd. It was as if the skin around the cut had predated the decomposition process. He'd never seen that before. However, the old woman's hands were not cut. In fact, the rest of her body was bruised and broken. Her hands seemed to shine through unscathed. Walking over to her, he knelt down and lifted her hand. Already, he could smell the same pungent odor. The smell, now mixed with his latex gloves, is how his memory finally connected to the scent.

Years ago, when he was still just a rookie investigator, he recalled a scene where a man suddenly passed away at the dining room table. The man's wife stated that one minute he was eating his food, the next he keeled over and died. She was distraught, and he tried to comfort her.His partner and mentor handed him the wine glass he was drinking from and told him to smell it. It was this same scent that he was smelling now.

The next thing he knew, his partner was walking the wife out in cuffs. Later, he learned that this smell was poison. The same smell he was catching wafts of now.

Now that he determined it was a poison, he had to figure out why. He looked at the broken roses on the ground. The leaves were perfect, as were the petals. None were eaten by bugs. Despite being ripped from their stem, they still managed to bloom. Also, each rose had the reminiscent scent of the poison upon it. It was the same with the old woman's hands, which were calloused yet very clean.

Could it be that she applied this to the roses? Then an image popped into his mind of that murderous wife's flower beds. Her hobby was gardening, and she had a beautiful bed of flowers. *Who knew her passion for creating such beautiful life would lead to death.*

Now, he took several steps backward to observe the whole crime scene. In his mind, he could see what happened. Now, he understood how the poison entered their skin. In the end, the roses gained their vengeance, proving that roses are as beautiful as they are deadly. However, despite the solution of the larger mystery, something still troubled the lead authority.

The murderous band of vendors, died as a result of the poison. That's not what bothers me. What truly bothered him was that their bodies had almost completely decomposed. *This couldn't have been the cause of the poison. That wouldn't have affected them in such a way.* That's when he heard the whisper. He didn't know where it was coming from… it was so soft that it could hardly be heard at all.

"Codladh anois mo lomhara. Alainn ta sin a eile, fanacht an ag ardu ghrian."

It was a woman singing in a strange tongue. He looked down at The Old Lady Who Sold Roses. Her lips did not move, but he had an odd feeling that he was hearing her. Later, he would ask if anyone else heard it, but no one did. To this day, he often thinks back to that moment and wonders if he had truly heard the singing or if there had been some semblance of truth about the craft of The Old Lady Who Sold The Roses.

****

How, then, did the murderous group die? Was it witchcraft? Were they genuinely cursed, as they had suspected? I assure you that this tale of macabre is much more benign. It wasn't the responsibility of the supernatural, and the old lady was not a witch, as she had once been suspected. Rather, it was a tale of consequential madness.

Each night, The Lady Who Sold The Roses sang a song in a strange tongue. In fact, it was a song taught to her by her grandmother in Gaelic. As a young girl, her grandmother taught her that if she spoke and sang to the plants, they would have the desire to be more beautiful. If the others had known the words, they might not have been so hasty, for the song translated was: "Sleep now, my precious. Beautiful are those who rest, awaiting the rising sun."

What of the deaths of the other vendors? Everyone had failed to see that there was a large jar that the old woman kept on the shelf below her front table. This jar contained a liquid that promoted quick growth and prevented insect attacks and plant diseases. It was a recipe passed through her family from one generation to the next. It was extremely effective; however, it was highly poisonous to humans. Each night she took extra care to rub the solution on every branch and budding leaf with total concentration so that she would not cut herself.

Then, each morning, she was greeted with beautiful, abundant roses. However, the others failed to understand because they also failed to befriend her. Instead, they made murderous plans grown out of their own jealousy. For years, their madness manifested in anger and frustration. It only took

114

one evening when the wind blew just right to carry her voice in their direction, causing them to aim their frustration.

So be warned: one should never foster anger or frustration, for nature has a balance. She will reward those who uphold it but punish those who go against it.

GHOST TOUR

Just another item off my bucket list thought Thomas. Standing in a semi-large crowd waiting for the ghost tour to start. It was the renowned Ghastly Ghost Tours of New Orleans. According to their brochures, this was the only genuine, authentic tour. It brought you through the famous streets of Bourbon and Dauphine, and told the real tragedies that led to their second life as apparitions. Thomas could not wait. They met in front of Reverend Zombie's Voodoo Shop, and he watched as the noisy procession of a jazz wedding marched down the street. Each person held a drink in their hand and danced to the jazz musicians who led the husband and his bride down the streets in a drunkenly staggered sway.

Thomas looked at each tour attendee. Half the people were smiling, while the other half looked bored at hearing the drudgeries of days long forgotten. He didn't care, though, because this was his night. It was the moment he had dreamed of for years. In short, Thomas was a paranormal enthusiast. For years, Thomas had watched every episode of any show that told true ghost stories or hauntings. He greedily consumed each story, video, or picture the Internet had to offer about real ghosts. Undoubtedly, every few stories came from Louisiana, which, in turn, made this a must-visit vacation destination.

Thomas was a mediocre-looking single man. That was, save for his long, spindly fingers that were well out of proportion with the rest of his body. He was in his thirties with a small bald patch surrounded by his dark brown medium-length hair that went wild as the rare breeze came through St. Peter Street. Standing in the New Orleans heat and sun, his bald spot turned crimson. Desperately, he desired to scratch this burnt portion of his head with his spider fingers, but he knew that if he did, it would hurt. He raised his hand to shoulder level and then let it fall again. That's when he saw her, and instantly, the rest of his face turned crimson, resembling a volcano in the first stages of lava flow.

Pink lips first flashed in the setting sun, catching his attention. Her hair was blonde, but so light that it almost appeared to have no color. This, of course, wasn't natural. She wore heavy makeup and thick black eyeliner. To him, she was different, and she was what he was looking for in a woman. Style-wise, she was Goth, but there was something different about her. He realized that he had been staring. She caught his gaze for a second and smiled at him. This made him die a little inside, but not in a bad way. She turned and tried to squeeze through the crowd, walking in his direction. Inside, he began to panic. Thomas hadn't exactly had a lot of practice with women. Usually, he cracks under pressure by making some stupid comments.

Sweat began to pour as she approached him, but she showed no sign of slowing. Instead, she continued past him as if she had walked right through him. At least, that's how Thomas felt. Once again, his heart was crushed. He was mistaken. She was looking at someone behind him. She never even noticed his existence.

"That was brutal," someone said to his right.

Turning to look with a bit of chagrin, he replied, "I'm sorry?"

"I watched that whole thing," she laughed.

It was a woman, and she was fairly pretty. She stood looking at him with a warm smile that formed between two cherry-red lips. She looked quite ordinary, which wasn't Thomas's taste at all, with a plain red T-shirt and blue jean shorts. Even so, she was a woman, and she noticed Thomas. She was even talking to him.

"Don't worry, that happens to all of us! Especially me," she said.

"Yeah, well, I wouldn't have known what to say to her even if she did want to talk to me." Instantly, he regretted saying it. He wanted to impress her, but despite being in the French Quarter, he hadn't had a drop to drink. So, he was still quite uptight. "I mean, um… what brings you to the ghost tour?"

"Well, honestly?"

"Honestly, your husband probably dragged you into coming. Where is he?" Thomas just expected it out of someone who looked so homely.

"Actually, I'm no longer married," she said with a smile, raising her left hand and portraying a pale band of skin around her third finger. Evidence of where a ring once sat.

"Sorry."

"No problem, but a long story," she smiled that same pretty smile again, and Thomas' cheeks flushed, betraying his stone face. "Actually, he was a jerk. Cheated on me, but I left with the house and the car." She paused and smiled for a second. "Actually, it's a shorter story than I thought!" Then she laughed, and it was a genuine laugh.

"I know what you mean," Thomas remarked.

"Oh, you were married once?"

"Huh?" Thomas was confused for a second. "Oh no, sorry. I meant, like, I know, but I don't really know because I have never been married. But I can imagine, or at least, I suppose that I could imagine. I'm going to stop talking now."

"No, you're fine. That was sweet of you to say. Sweet and confusing, but sweet none-the-less." To Thomas, she was the sweet one. Thomas desperately wanted to latch onto her already. She continued, "I've had a rough couple of months, but I finally learned to let that go and do something I've always wanted to do; go on a ghost tour!" she explained.

Thomas's mind stuttered to describe just how excited he felt. The words 'more alive' might come close.

"Really? You've always wanted to go on a ghost tour?" He was used to being the only one with a strong interest in the paranormal. *Finally, I found someone else who shared my interests, and it's a girl!*

"Oh yeah! It's been on my bucket list for years!" She laughed loudly, and people gave her strange looks, but she dismissed them. "I'm always reading books about it, and I love those ghost-hunting shows! New Orleans is like the paranormal capital of the U.S."

"Oh my gosh, me too! I've waited for years to do this. In fact, I..." he was cut off.

"Alright, everyone on the tour, please gather closely. I am your ghost host with the most! Welcome everyone to the most authentic, historical ghost tour that New Orleans has to offer!" He said this most theatrically, really acting out everything he said. The tour guide had half of his head shaven while the other half acted as a side part where his medium-length hair gathered resting on his head. He swung around a black cane with silver trim as he spoke. "My name is Enzo, and I will cordially be your guide. Ladies and gentlemen, if you will please, follow me this way. Also, this is your last chance to escape." Smiling, he bowed and turned, whipping his cane into the air like a marching band's baton. He held the air of a conductor leading the deaf. Everyone gathered silently and succinctly into line falling for his charm. The leader of a black parade if you will.

Thomas looked over to finish his statement, but the group had already started walking. He hurried along with them in fear of being left behind. He looked over at the woman he just met, and he could see the eagerness on her face, too. She smiled a lovely smile at him.

"By the way, my name is Lynne."

"Hi Thomas, my name is Lynne. Wait, no!" He instantly smacked himself on the forehead. "I mean that I'm Thomas, of course."

"I got it," she smiled. "You're cute."

Instantly, his face was beet red. Those were not words that people generally used to describe him. He just wanted to latch onto her and never let her go. Tonight was a good night. He hadn't felt so lively in such a long time. Usually, no one ever noticed him, but this time, he had the attention of a beautiful woman.

Darkness began to creep in as the sun drew to a close upon the French Quarter. The old-style French buildings with balconies and intricate shutters cast long shadows on the street below. Enzo, the ghost tour guide, gathered the crowd around the side of a building. Everyone came in close. People awkwardly lined up as they were not sure where to stand.

"Come on in, people, I don't bite… hard." He said this with a devious smile. Some of the women playfully cooed at the remark. "Okay, let me lay the ground rules for this tour. Everyone stay close together in a group! I do not want to lose anyone. I can honestly say I have never lost anyone on a tour, and I would like to keep this impeccable record. Ghosts have been seen on this tour, and sometimes, they have been known to beckon people to take a closer look. I advise that you do not do this! I will take you to several places and tell you true stories of ghosts and the macabre. New Orleans has a rich history from the early settlements of the French all the way through modern day. Any questions?

Thomas quickly raised his hand and waited to be called on. Enzo looked around the crowd and looked right past Thomas.

"Okay then, if there are no questions, then please follow me!" Enzo said and took off down the sidewalk.

Bummed and agitated that he was so blatantly ignored. Thomas shrugged it off and began to walk down the sidewalk.

"What a jerk!" Lynne said to Thomas.

"Eh, it's okay," he replied. "It was a dumb question anyway."

"Well, just ask it at the next stop."

"Okay."

Traversing down the bricked streets, they came to a traditional mansion. It was sandwiched between two other buildings angled on a corner. It had dark trim with onyx-colored pillars down the front supporting a wrought iron balcony. It was as beautiful as it was ominous, its shadows creeped across the street toward them. Darkness swept in with the setting sun, but the crowds continued to grow on the streets around them. Nighttime was infamously busier than daytime in New Orleans. It was just the nature of the party capital of the world.

"This, ladies and gentlemen, is 1801 Dauphine Street," Enzo began. "Does anyone know why this building is significant?"

Thomas spoke up eagerly, "It's Marie Laveau's house!"

"Anyone at all?" Enzo repeated, completely ignoring Thomas's comment.

Lynne grew a bit agitated and spoke up on Thomas's behalf. "This is Marie Laveau's house."

"That is correct!" Enzo congratulated her, "Well done, Madame. She is correct. This is the Voodoo Queen's home. She was a nasty one, this Ms. Laveau was." He continued talking about her misdeeds and what the house was used for.

Once again, Thomas was disheartened and even more agitated. Lynne looked at him and smiled again. She touched his arm as a reassurance and then nodded to him. Silently apologizing for what happened.

Enzo finished his monologue about the fearful Ms. Laveau and her misdeeds. Then, he once again began walking down Dauphine Street. Hanging his head, Thomas reluctantly followed the group. Taking one last look at the Laveau house, Thomas turned his head and could clearly see a woman in a dark dress staring back at him. Instantly, this shot chills down his spine. He tapped on Lynne's shoulder.

"Yeah?" she asked, turning toward him.

Pointing back at the balcony, Thoms asked her, "Do you see her?"

She looked, but the balcony was empty. "Where, on the balcony?"

"Yes. A… a woman in a dark-colored dress," he looked back, but she was gone. "She was just right there."

"A ghost, perhaps?"

His, the tingles turned into butterflies. "Yes! It must have been." Now, he was smiling. "She was right there staring at me. It was hard to tell, but she could have been wearing period-type clothing. Almost like from the 1800s."

"Oh wow," she smiled, "I'm jealous!"

"Yeah," he laughed, "I guess it was a little freakier than I thought it would be."

"It's not so scary when you see it on a screen," Lynne replied.

"Hey, keep up with group!" someone shouted. They had fallen behind. It was likely Enzo who shouted, but it was hard to tell.

They looked at each other and giggled. They walked quickly to catch up with the group. They cut over to Bourbon Street. Already, the crowds had grown, and at this point, the shadows had ceased to exist. Night finally arrived, which meant the party had just begun. It was still premature, and the streets weren't yet packed with the loathsome creatures that usually came.

"To your left, ladies and gentlemen, is the Lafitte Blacksmith Shop Bar. This is by far the oldest building in New Orleans. However, we are not going to be talking about that. Instead, we are going to talk about the Lafitte Guest House." Enzo used his hands to display the multiple-floor lodging house that used to be a luxurious mansion. Once again, there was a balcony where people often stood coaxing women in exchange for beads. Each person in the group admired the beauty of this building.

Lynne and Thomas stood; mouths agape at the beauty of it. They were squeezed out to the back of the crowd listening to the story. It was about an unfortunate wife and mother who lost her whole family to a plague. It turned out she was a caring ghost who makes sure to cover up her guests at night, then leave a cold, wet kiss upon their foreheads. Enzo wrapped up the story with his usual dramatic flair by swinging his fancy cane up into the air and catching it.

The crowd gathered again to follow him down Bourbon Street. Lynne began to follow them. Thomas, however, hung back and stared at the balcony. He hoped to catch a glimpse of the caring ghost who attended to her guests at the LaFitte. A few seconds passed, and there was nothing. So, he ran to catch up with the group. As he turned to walk away, the woman he saw at the Lavaeu house now stood in his path. He fell backward as he tried to avoid walking right into her.

Horror vibrated through him. Every hair, every goose pimple, every hallowed breath seemed to stand on end as impending death drew closer, he could now see clearly that her eyes were hollow. There was nothing in her sockets, and blood ran down from her eyelids to her chin, dripping to the ground. Her mouth was open as if she were screaming. Her teeth were jagged and unclean. Her hair was done up in the fashion of the 1800s with a small hat pinned into her hair. Also, her dress wasn't made of dark colors; instead, it was just old and wet giving it the appearance of being dark. In fact, at one time, that dress had held a vibrant, magnificent color, but due to its current state, it appeared in shades of gray. Her hand jutted out from her body as if she was trying to grab him. Some of her fingernails were long, and others were broken off.

Thomas turned away, for the sheer horror of it terrified him. He couldn't handle looking into those hollow, soulless eyes any longer. He shielded his face with his hand and mumbled incomprehensible sounds of terror. No hand touched him, though. Nothing happened. When he peeked through his fingers, he realized the woman was gone. Dropping his hand, he surveyed the immediate area. She was nowhere to be seen. He saw only people walking around with drinks in their hands.

Relieved that the horror was done, Thomas sat up. He had always wanted to see a ghost, but never like that. Nothing like this happened during those shows he watched; only in horror movies. *Nonetheless, it is happening to me, but why? Who was she? Why was she following me?* A thousand questions came to his mind, but then he realized that the tour had gone on without him.

He found the tour in time to watch them turn the corner and go back toward Dauphine Street. He started running after them out of fear of losing the group or, even worse, being alone. Lynne was too busy following the group to notice that Thomas was behind. He watched as she disappeared behind the corner of the building.

Nervously, he ran after the group, but the streets were crowded. No cars drove down them anymore, but it seemed like more people kept flooding in out of nowhere. Finally, he reached the same street where the tour headed. He looked up to see the old-style street sign, which read Dumaine Street. Turning right, he saw the last of the group go that way. He picked up his pace but slowed to a brisk walk as he noticed rather strange-looking people on this street.

It was dark. The street was pinned rather closely by buildings and just a few street lights. In the shadows, Thomas saw a dark silhouette of a small group of people. They moved in odd ways as if they couldn't hold still. They bobbed up and down in a broken rhythm. Warily, he walked past them, trying not to make eye contact. Suddenly, they all plunged down upon him, grabbing him from every angle! He regretted ever coming to New Orleans. Their touch felt cold, as they grabbed onto whatever they could. It was the most overwhelming sensation he had ever felt. At last, he shouted and wriggled himself free of their grip.

These were not normal people. They were only shadows of people who used to be. They weren't alive. They hid in the shadows of the buildings. His terror swelled as he realized that their numbers continued to grow. He ran, dodging their attempts to grab him, and pushed the ones in his way. With all his strength, he clawed through them for dear life. Finally, he spilled out onto the well-lit Dauphine Street in a crumpled heap.

Those fragmented souls remained between the buildings, and he could hear their high-pitched wails of failure. Desperately trying to catch his breath, Thomas embraced the glowing street lights on the Dauphine. People passed him without notice. *I suppose it isn't uncommon for people to lie in the streets of New Orleans. The difference is, that I haven't had a drop of*

He got to his feet and searched desperately for the tour. Just a short way down the street, he could see them standing on the corner of Dauphine and Orlean. Everybody was looking at a large French-style mansion that sat on the corner. Enzo stood in front, talking in his eccentric manner, telling a story.

Thomas finally caught his breath, and ran, trying to meet back up with the group. Tonight's experiences had been terrifying, but a part of him found them to be a bit exhilarating too. *Well, isn't this what you came down here for?* He slowed to a fast walk. It didn't take him long to discreetly find his way back into the group. No one had even noticed his arrival except Lynne.

"Where'd you go?" Lynne asked him, worried.

"Sorry, I got sidetracked," he said.

"You saw more ghosts, didn't you?" she asked him excitedly.

"Yes," his reply was half excitement and half terror.

"Oh, you suck!" she said, clearly jealous. "I haven't even seen a single one yet!"

"Shush!" Someone from the tour hushed them and gave them a weird look.

"Sorry," Lynne whispered. They turned to listen to the tail end of Enzo's story.

"So, the Sultan had grandiose parties, and it was reported they had wild orgies in his home. Now, I know what you're thinking. How do I get in on that? Ha! You wouldn't be so interested if you knew what befell this mansion. Purportedly, he actually was *not* the Sultan! Rather, he was the Sultan's brother who took off with the family's wealth. Fleeing, he took the money to America, where he bought this beautiful mansion. However, ladies and gentlemen, that is not the weirdest part of the story.

"Apparently, one morning, the neighbors awoke to find blood running down the front porch steps. When the police showed up, they found a most grotesque scene. The story goes that the night before, a wild party was in full swing at the Sultan's place. This was typical. There was hardly a night that a party wasn't held. That was when multiple people in Arab garb entered the party and murdered all the partygoers inside.

"These murderers cut the partygoers into small pieces and scattered them about the house. Inside was a bloodbath of torn limbs. Carpets and curtains were stained red. Not to mention, the coroner had a most disturbing jigsaw puzzle trying to put the pieces back together to determine who the victims were. In the courtyard behind the house, they found a hand sticking out from a grave... as if it were reaching for life itself. This, my friends, was the Sultan. Although the mystery was never truly solved, they believe the true Sultan discovered where his brother was and ordered the massacre. It remains haunted to this day. There are reports that the walls bleed, the floors seep blood, and the sounds of grand parties still pervade these rooms." Enzo finished telling the story, stepped aside, and presented the house.

"Enzo? Do people ever report being attacked by shadow creatures in the dark streets of New Orleans?" Thomas wanted to know more about those creatures he just experienced. He could barely wait for Enzo to finish so he could ask about it.

"Do you hear that?" he said, looking at the crowd. "Is it the sound of a party?" Enzo smiled.

"Enzo! Did you hear my question?" Thomas was now even more agitated. He saw others raise their hands like they had questions, too, including Lynne, who was trying to help Thomas.

"We are close to being done," Enzo said. He turned to Thomas and Lynne. "Please hold your questions until the end. Thanks!"

Lynne's face grew grim, and she started to walk toward Enzo like she might start a confrontation.

"Lynne," Thomas stopped her. "Please don't. I'll just wait until the tour is over."

"What a jerk!" she said. "Are you sure?"

"Yes, I'm sure," he said. "Technically, I interrupted his story. I thought he was done. Let's try to stay with the group."

"Okay," she replied, then turned to follow the rest of the tour.

Thomas started to follow until he heard someone call out.

"Hey!"

Thomas looked around but didn't see anyone. Then he looked back at the Sultan's palace and saw a man standing in the doorway. The door was open, and he was trying to get Thomas' attention, motioning him to come closer. Thomas looked back to the group. They were getting ahead of him again.

"Me?" Thomas asked, pointing to himself.

"Yeah, you," the man said. "Come here."

Thomas looked back and saw the group getting even farther away down Dauphine Street. He needed to make a decision. This guy was strange-looking and was dressed in Middle Eastern clothes. *Perhaps this might be a part of the tour, connected to the story about the Sultan.* I guess I could take a minute to see what the guy wants.

As he walked up to the front steps, Thomas began to get an eerie feeling that something was not right. The man continued to beckon him to the door. The closer he got to this man, the more Thomas began to question who he was. He wore baggy clothing tucked in at all the cuffs and at the waist. His face looked like an Arabic man's. However, he seemed pale, like he was sick. Red rings around his eyes accentuated his ghastly appearance.

"What do you want?" Thomas asked as he stopped at the bottom of the stairway.

The man's eyes suddenly lost all color, and his pupils clouded. He let out a horrifying moan and pointed down. Thomas looked where he pointed and watched as blood ran down the staircase. Quickly, he picked up his feet to avoid drenching them in the liquid satin. He looked to the top of the stairs, but the man had vanished. The door remained open, but the man was nowhere to be found.

"Aii!" A screech came from behind him.

Swirling around, Thomas saw that the horrifying lady in the dress had returned. Her eyes were even more hollow and darker than before. Long, spindly hands with sharp, filed-down nails jetted out in front of her. Thomas turned back to the Sultan's palace to see that the blood on the stairs was gone. The door was still open.

Thinking this was his only means of escape from the evil spirit, Thomas ran up the once-bloodied staircase. He rushed through the door, turned, and slammed it just in time to see the lady's face on the threshold. With a breath of relief, he laid his back against the door, trying to guard it as if a door could stop her from entering the house.

After a few seconds of silence, he eased up and walked into the house. It seemed rather modern. The lights were on, and he walked into a modern hallway with modern amenities. He expected a more classic, older look to the house based on the stories and how that man was dressed. In fact, the house was done entirely in a modern Western fashion. Not a spot of Middle Eastern flare anywhere to be seen.

"Hello?" Thomas called out. His voice echoed through the empty hallways.

No reply.

"Is anyone here?" he shouted again. "I'm terribly sorry to barge in like this, but I had nowhere else to go!"

No reply again. All was silent in the house. No stirring, no noise of active participation. Not even the noises that usually accompany old houses like this one. It was strange. It was downright unnatural. The silence surrounded Thomas like a shroud of nothingness encapsulating him within the horror he had made.

Suddenly, he heard a twang. *That came from the living room.* He heard it again. Arabic sitar music filled the air. It filled every hall. Every crack and nook within the house reverberated with exuberant music. This was a welcome change to the silence, but it was unsettling in the nothingness. That's when he began to hear the voices of many people. The chatter grew louder until he couldn't hear anything else. He walked down the hallway and turned into the living room. To his amazement, he saw a crowd of people. A band sat on giant pillows playing Arabic-style music, and a lively party ensued. It was odd. It felt like walking into the past.

The room was lit by gas lamps. People shouted and giggled. Women were dressed in an Arabic fashion while others strode around topless, being chased by shameless wealthy men. The living room was packed, and in the center was a man dressed in wealthy clothing sitting on a rich satin pillow. This pillow had frilling sewn onto the edges. The man wore a white Middle Eastern suit from head to toe. He looked like a prince from a Hollywood movie. He shouted praise for the music. Everyone danced.

There were countless devious acts of lust in every corner of the room. Thomas was ashamed to look at them. Each person seemed intoxicated by the perfume in the air, among other influences. However, no one cared what anyone else did. Everyone seemed to do just as they pleased, and no one was the wiser. No one dared judge because everyone was doing something. This was the essence of a harem.

Thomas looked back at the front door as men opened the door and tried to walk in quietly. They were obviously of Arabic descent, but they had a murderous look on their faces. Thomas knew what was happening. Surely, he was witnessing a re-enactment of the terrible story Enzo had just told.

"Everyone! You need to run!" shouted Thomas, but the harem did not notice him. They continued their sinful acts, paying no attention to the warning bell.

What happened next was odd. Thomas watched as the scene faded in and out like a television with bad reception. It only appeared briefly to show bits and pieces. Even so, the bits and pieces were gruesome, terrible, inconceivable things to witness. One moment, everyone was partying. The next, some were dead. Then, more were dead. Now, all were dead. Save only the wealthy man still sitting on the satin pillow, now stained with blood.

They took the wealthy man by his arms and dragged him outside. He was yelling in a different language, but his tone was pleading. That desperation is universal in all languages. The back door flew open, and Thomas watched as the flicker from the past to the present appeared in flashes. They disappeared into the courtyard. Carefully, Thomas walked to the back door and opened it. The men were gone, and there was no trace of the wealthy man. The area was vacant, except for the hand that stuck out of the ground.

That's when Thomas heard it. It started like a muffled whine. *That must be coming from the man they buried.* He ran to what he thought must be a grave in a panic. The muffled whine grew louder and more desperate. Still, the hand did not move.

"Are you still alive?" Thomas shouted.

All he heard was the same panicked, muffled noise. Still, the hand did not move. He poked at it, trying to see if he could evoke a response. However, the hand only moved when it was poked, not of its own accord. *Where is that muffled sound coming from?* Slowly, he laid his head on the ground next to the hand and listened. He realized that this muffled voice was repeating the something. He couldn't make it out, so he leaned in closer and listened more intently. Suddenly, the hand grabbed his shoulder.

Thomas screamed and tried desperately to pull out of the hand's grip. Bits of Earth crumbled around the hand as Thomas pulled with all his might. With fear as his fulcrum, Thomas pulled so hard that he pulled this man out of the grave! Dirt and sod separated apart in heaps as he rose from the grave. Thomas continued to shout as he tried to scramble backward, but the hand was too strong. The man was covered in dirt. His face was bloodied and torn apart. Paralyzed with fear, Thomas fell onto his back, and the corpse fell on top of him.

"You are dead!" shouted the corpse. His voice was grim and dark with a rasp that was absolutely terrifying.

"No!" Thomas retorted as if he had a choice.

"You are dead!"

Thomas shut his eyes and gave up, totally gave up, waiting for the eventuality of death to set in. Nothing happened. He opened his eyes, and the corpse was gone. He was lying on his back in the courtyard, but the grass beneath him was undisturbed. Wasting no more time, he got up and ran to the house. It was once again restored to its modern quiet state. No more partying ghosts. No harem.

Thomas ran out the door and back onto Dauphine Street. He was thankful to be out of that nightmare. He decided that he was done seeing ghosts. Never had he thought that he would encounter so many of them. He decided that from this day on, his obsessions with the paranormal and ghosts would stop. Looking left and right, he desperately searched for where the tour may have gone. He wanted to catch up to them and Lynne.

Meanwhile, the tour arrived at its final destination, Jackson Square. This park was not too far from where the tour began on St. Peter Street. Exhausted, each person took a seat on one of the benches. Even Enzo sat, laying his walking cane upon his lap. Lynne didn't know where Thomas was, and she became increasingly concerned.

"Alright, ladies and gentlemen, we have come to the end of our terror tour," Enzo smiled at everyone. "Do not fret, though; we still have one last story."

"Wait!" Lynne shouted as she raised her hand. "We are missing someone!"

"What?" Enzo shouted, puzzled. He shot up out of his seat. Then, with his finger, he counted the group. Finally, after walking through the crowd, he ended his count at twenty-three.

"We seem to have everyone," he said as he looked at Lynne strangely.

"Wait!" she hollered, stood up, and scanned the crowd. "No, we don't. Thomas is missing. The last time I saw him was at the Sultan's place. We have to go back and find him!" She got up, determined to look for him with or without the group's help.

Thomas ran through the streets of New Orleans. He was panicking. *I have to get back to the group.* Something inside told him that they were at Jackson Park. He tried to weave in and out of the crowded roads, searching desperately for the road leading to the park. Finally, he could see the park entrance and the folks gathered around Enzo. He could also see Lynne.

She seemed upset. He was still at least a block away.

"Lynne!" he shouted to her. "I'm back here!"

She didn't hear him. No one could. A dark alleyway separated him from the group sitting at the park. He felt increasingly nervous about this alleyway, aside from the fact that it was almost pitch-black inside. There was a malevolent presence there. *Could it be that woman again?* He decided to chance it… he had to get back to Lynne.

"I'm coming," he shouted, "I'll make it this time!"

Quickly, he tried to walk down the alleyway. There was no time to waste. The darkness played tricks on his eyes. The end seemed to get longer and longer. He felt that with every step he took, three steps were added to the end of the alley. That's when he tripped and fell flat on his face.

He tried to stand, but his foot was snagged on something. It was impossible to make out what it was in the darkness. He reached his hand down to free himself from whatever ensnared him. He felt a few long, tube-like things wrapping around his ankle. He tried to pull them off, to get free, but that's when he realized they weren't just strange tube-like things; they were fingers!

A hand grabbed his ankle, causing him to fall. He screamed and began to kick at it with his other foot. Finally, he was able to free himself. He got back up and began to run. Now, hands popped out of the darkness from every angle, desperately trying to trap him. Some snatched at his arms, while others gripped his legs and feet. He was able to fend them off with a short burst of speed, but he realized that he wouldn't be making it down the alley. There were far too many of them.

Slowly, they grew out of the darkness and began to take forms in the shadows. *These are the same nightmare creatures that I experienced earlier!* Suddenly, one appeared right in front of him, blocking his view of Lynne and the others on the tour. He ran directly into it. It was the biggest of the creatures he'd seen that night. It instantly wrapped its black arms around Thomas. It had an iron grip. Thomas couldn't move. He looked like he was being hugged by a black silhouette.

From around its head, Thomas looked for Lynne and could see her still standing with the group. He longed to be by her. To attach to her and to be with her. This desire welled up from the deepest parts of his soul. His strong emotions boiled to the surface, and he shouted, "Lynne!"

Honey brown hair flew out as Lynne spun her head to look back. "What was that?" she whispered.

Enzo gave Lynne a funny smirk. "Oh really, and what was this person's name? If you don't mind me asking?"

"His name is Thomas," she shouted, "Now, shouldn't you have him on your list or something?"

Everyone looked at her strangely.

"Did anyone else see this, Thomas?" Enzo asked the rest of the group.

Everyone shook their heads 'no.'

"He asked you questions, and you completely ignored him," she said. "He walked with me and stood by me most of the time. How could no one else notice?" Lynne was becoming frantic. She had grown fond of Thomas. "Is this some kind of a sick joke?"

"Ladies and gentlemen," Enzo gathered everyone's attention. "I have come to my final ghost story of the night."

Lynne didn't understand what he was doing. "Hey! We need to go find him. He could be hurt!"

"Ma'am, there were only twenty-three in the group, and twenty-three are still here. If you would please have a seat, I may be able to help." Enzo said calmly as if he'd dealt with panicking people before.

Due to his calm demeanor and ability to command authority, Lynne sat down. She felt there was nothing else she could do. Still, she hoped Thomas would find them.

"As I was saying, we have come to our final story of the night," Enzo said congenially. "Years ago, a tour remarkably similar to ours was called the *Ghastly Ghost Tours*. However, the company, sadly, went under… about ten years ago. There is a reason why I caution everyone so strongly about becoming separated from the group. Because on their last tour, they lost someone."

Chills shot down Lynne's spine. *Could this really be happening?* The mere thought of it was unbelievable. She tried hard to think back. He was continually ignored when asking questions. *What about when I first saw him? Did that girl walk past him, or did she walk right through him?* Lynne was standing at a weird angle and couldn't be sure. *There is no way that could be true!*

"Lynne, correct?" Enzo said, snapping her out of her thoughts.

"S-sorry what?" she stuttered.

"You said his name was Thomas, correct?" Enzo asked.

"Uh-huh, he said he had been waiting his whole life to go on this tour. He was really excited about it. We both were, actually." Her gaze fixed on the sidewalk.

"Wow," Enzo said, astonished. "You may want to stay seated as I tell you this."

Lynne swallowed hard.

"Thomas Brecken was a man of mediocre status in every way possible. He was someone who played it safe his whole life. However, he had a strange fascination; some would've called it an obsession with the paranormal. He waited years to come down to New Orleans, and the *Ghost Tour* was at the top of his bucket list!"

Lynne was shocked. It sounded just like the Thomas she had met. *How could I not have known that he was a ghost? Could this truly be happening?*

"*The Ghastly Ghost Tours* was the top-ranked ghost tour in New Orleans. Naturally, this is the one Thomas chose for his ghost tour. It was a trip of a lifetime. A trip where he came to find himself and hoped to find the woman of his dreams. Someone, anyone, who would pay him attention. Someone like Lynne over here," he used his cane to point to Lynne.

Her face flushed red with embarrassment.

"Sorry Lynne. He must have wandered off after one of the stops during the ghost tour. However, as usual, nobody noticed that he was missing. Finally, at the end of the tour, the guide gathered everyone around Jackson Park. Just as I did tonight and discovered one person was missing. The tour guide re-traced his steps, but the streets were so busy. He went back and checked with the hotels in the area. Luckily, they knew

Thomas was staying at one, so they were sure they'd find him. However, as the next day passed, he never checked out of the hotel. In fact, he never returned to get his stuff. The cops got involved, but Thomas never turned up. Never grabbed his stuff and never got on the plane for his return trip home. He simply vanished." Enzo's voice turned grave.

"After this, a lawsuit was filed against *The Ghastly Ghost Tours*. They couldn't afford the litigation, so the company went bankrupt. This is the reason we are so particular about not losing anyone. However, the legal allegation is not where this story ends. After the incident, people reported that a strange man would often attend the ghost tours. Sometimes, he would be seen peeking his head in during stories. Some tour guides saw him, too. It wasn't long before he became known as the Ghost Tour Phantom. Every so often, on my tours, he comes through. Usually, it's just someone asking about the strange guy who walked up and listened to our tour. Sometimes, it is just someone hearing the voice of a man. You see, our ghost, Thomas, was doomed to go on the Ghost Tours repeatedly but never got to finish them. However, no one has ever mistaken him for a tour customer. Do you mind telling us about your experience tonight?"

Lynne's face flushed as red as an apple from the sudden spotlight. Everyone on the tour looked at her with great intrigue. All she wanted to do was cry because Thomas was more than just some phantom figure you pretended to see out of the corner of your eye. To her, he was real, and he wasn't all that different from Lynne herself. Shy, curious, and looking for an adventure. He just happened to get more than he bargained for. *I wonder if there is any way to help Thomas?* But she knew the truth. *Sadly, he is dead, and nothing can change that.* Suddenly, she realized that people were still staring at her, waiting for her to explain.

Bashful, she stuttered as she began the story. Being careful not to share too much, she told just the basics, leaving out the details regarding her feelings for Thomas. She admitted only to Thomas telling her his name and becoming concerned when she realized that he wasn't with the group anymore. She noticed the girl who walked through him earlier, listening intently. When she stopped her story, everyone seemed impressed.

Enzo took over at this point and used her experience to finish his final monologue. He made sure to kindly ask everyone for tips. Everyone began to scatter in different directions. Some hung around to talk with Enzo. Many cast their attention on Lynne. The tourists offered silent looks of disbelief or envy. She'd had enough of the tour for the night and decided it was time for her to leave.

It was oddly quiet on the streets of New Orleans as she returned to her hotel. The town felt eerie as she walked alone through the French Quarter. She had a strange sensation that someone was watching her, and she couldn't help but wonder where Thomas was now. That's when she heard a faint voice in the distance. Someone was calling her name in distress.

The sound was slightly distorted by all the buildings and businesses of the French Quarter. Still, it was unmistakable to her. Her innate motherly instincts came over her, and she began to panic as she tried to figure out the source. She had an overwhelming desire to comfort her caller. *It has to be Thomas.* Eventually, the streets went silent, and she returned to her hotel room.

That night, her thoughts haunted her, not because of her ghoulish encounter or fear of another encounter. Instead, she was haunted by the thoughts of Thomas and his ever-revolving nightmare. He never truly finished his tour, and each time, he just hoped someone would see him. Finally, she was able to fall asleep in her cozy hotel room but never forgot Thomas. Nor could she ever forget her first ghost tour.

****

Just another item off of his bucket list, thought Thomas as he stood with the group. He was ready to go on his first ghost tour. Shy, the sun peeked above the horizon, just about ready to usher in the darkness of the night. He looked around the crowd discreetly, hoping to find a woman who might be interested in him. Sadly, he had never been very good with the ladies, but he thought if there ever was a time, then it would be now. Many people stood around in groups. It seemed that there were a lot of couples on the tour that day. Then he saw her.

She was an older woman, possibly in her 60s, and she was looking directly at him. She seemed familiar to him and looked so kind. Although, she was a bit too old for his tastes. She smiled at him and he turned away out of shyness. However, her smile was warm and friendly.

Slowly, his head turned back, and he saw the older woman approach him. He turned and put his back to her hoping that she wouldn't come closer. It wasn't trying to be rude; he just didn't know what to say.

"Excuse me?" she said kindly and gently.

"Umm. Yes. Hi," said Thomas sheepishly.

"Do you remember me?" she asked him, smiling.

Confused, he tilted his head to the side awkwardly. "I'm sorry, Miss."

"Lynne," she offered.

"I'm sorry, Lynne." He stopped for a second, and an odd feeling of familiarity came over him. "I'm sorry, but I don't. Should I?" He was shocked. *What was she sixty? Still, she struck him as beautiful.*

Lynne reached out and grabbed his hand. It was a slow and calculated movement, as if she was scared she wouldn't be able to touch him. It worked. She grabbed his hand and held it tight. She gasped at how inhumanly cold he was and the pain she could feel from him.

Once again, her touch flooded his mind with familiarity, but Thomas just couldn't believe it.

"It's been over thirty years, Thomas," she said.

"I haven't even hit thirty yet. I don't know how that's possible. This is my first time here, taking this ghost tour. I have been waiting my whole life for this."

"I know, Thomas," she said, patting his hand. "I know."

This struck Thomas as odd but somehow, he believed her. He believed that she knew. He believed her that they had met before, too. However, his memory was fuzzy on the details of that meeting. His longing for attachment took hold now, and he squeezed her hand. It was so warm and full of life.

"Remember Thomas," she told him, gazing into his eyes.

He tried to break the stare, but his efforts were fruitless.

"Remember, never let go of my hand. No matter what you see. Not until we make it to the end of this tour. I'll explain everything then, but for now, do not let go of my hand." Lynne spoke to Thomas as if he were a child.

Being obedient and loving the feeling of her gentle skin on his, he nodded yes.

"Do you promise?"

"Yes, I promise," he replied, confused but compliant.

"Attention everyone! Our tour is about to begin. So, please take a step forward so I can get a head count," a man dressed in dark clothing said.

Both Lynne and Thomas stepped forward.

The man's head cocked to the side so violently that you might have guessed that he accidentally broke it. He looked directly at Lynne and Thomas.

"Lynne?" he said, perplexed. "I see that you are joining us for our tour today?" He noticed that she appeared to be holding something in her hands, but nothing was there. He looked at her strangely.

"Yes, Matt," she replied, patting Thomas's hand. "It seems I have finally found what I was looking for." She looked over at Thomas, and he smiled back at her with confusion.

Matt stared at her for a moment as he watched her shift her gaze to the left at nothing, but her focus didn't go far. It was like she was looking at something right in front of her. Something that, apparently, only she could see.

Lynne had been mustering with the tour groups for almost two decades but never joined the tour. She quietly stood in line and watched each group go off for the night, returning the next day to do the same.

There was something different about her tonight, and it made Matt smile. For the first time since he began giving tours, Lynne looked happy. She wore a wide grin, and her presence was warm. He knew this would be a memorable tour. He welcomed everyone with his normal swagger. However, he had an extra hop in his step tonight. For tonight, the tour seemed to hold promise instead of just dark memories of what had been.

BATTLE ON THE CHARTREUSE SEA

Green waves washed over the field as the wind pushed the long grass sporadically. A tempest had erupted on this vast emerald sea, casting a pall on the calm warmth of the sun just moments ago. Waves crashed upon each other, racing around the two warriors who stood quietly poised for battle. Squaring off, yet separated only by a few leagues, desperately, this deluge attempted to overtake the warriors, but their strength proved to subdue the surge to mere ripples.

Both warriors blasted toward each other, unsheathing their swords, forcing a gale to exhale in their wake. Lightning struck as the two swords met, sending a clap of thunder from the impact. Each held a murderous look as their noses were now only inches apart. They were in a deadlock as both warriors pushed with all their might. They were so evenly matched that neither one moved an inch. The only thing that moved was their shitagi and hakama, disturbed by each gust of wind.

Violent fury forced them both backward several feet due to the explosion of energy that revolted outward from the clash. The impact of this energy would've knocked ordinary men off their feet, but these were samurai; perfect warriors of ancient Japan. The chartreuse sea, still erupting with raging rushes, overlooked the castle of Edo. They stood on an elevated expanse of grassy plain just outside of the main center of medieval Japan.

One warrior with untied, messy black hair looked at his opponent and smiled, "Well you're not the garbage fighter that I thought you were."

With wrath in his eye, the samurai with short, sandy-brown hair smiled. "I'm glad I impressed you, but you should know I've hardly begun to fight."

"Ha!" A short burst of a reply was all the response that was needed. His messy hair was just the start of his ensemble. His shitagi hung loosely around his chest, and his hakama was horribly wrinkled, falling just short of his ankles. He dug in his straw sandals, tamping down the green grass under his weight.

With a calmness through the storm, the other samurai stood with a strikingly different appearance. His short, sandy-brown hair was perfectly shaped and neatly done. There wasn't a single hair that dared stray. His dress followed, the shitagi nicely pressed and tucked into his uwa-obi. Below his belt hung the hakama with no noticeable wrinkles. It hung neatly at ankle level.

The wild samurai dashed forth again, and the two slashed and parried several times. Each one seemed to take turns on the offensive while the other defended. It was difficult to follow the wild samurai's movements. He was sporadic and uncontrolled. Meanwhile, the calm samurai's movements were filled with beauty, calculation, and precision. The two styles were perfect compliments of each other.

Pushing back, both warriors stopped to catch their breath.

Unexpectedly, six other samurai ran up the hill to reach the plain of green waves. They could see the two samurai and noticed that they tamed the waves by trampling the green grass in the shape of their thong sandals. The men had already unsheathed their swords. The group looked between the two in exasperation until the largest of the men spoke.

"On the orders of Edo Castle, I cannot allow the two of you to leave this place," he instructed them.

"Ah, you must be the castle's Royal Guard then?" Cool and collected was the voice of the well-put-together samurai.

"Yes," the man replied, "and we have been tasked with stopping you both. Even if that means killing you." A devilish smile appeared on his face.

"Is that so?" the cocky disheveled samurai said. "Well, this is about to get interesting."

"I agree," chimed in the calm one. "To be fair, I should probably fight five of them myself. Don't worry, I'll avenge your death after one takes you out."

"What is this now?" the leader of the Royal Guard raged.

"You're funny," the cocky one replied. "I'll take my three. Besides, I wouldn't want you to be too tired because I intend to finish our fight after this."

"Sounds like a plan," answered the calm one.

"Men," shouted the leader, "Split up! I'll take two with me, and you three take the other one!"

The samurais were surrounded. It was three to one on each samurai, but they weren't intimidated. Two tidal waves broke out in the tall green grass. In a flash undetectable to the untrained eye, the samurais stood on the outside of the triangle of guards who had once surrounded them. Blood dripped from their swords.

Wide-eyed and mouths agape, the Royal Guards stood frozen in their fighting stances. Suddenly, each sword broke in half and the men fell to the ground. Crimson sprayed the green waves red. The wind blew again as the swords dropped onto the flora below. The guards were dead.

The samurai whiped the blood off their katanas as they returned their attention to each other.

"Now, where were we?" the cocky samurai said as he looked at his opponent.

"I believe you were about to bow out of the fight after seeing that I am the superior fighter," the calm one said in a deep voice.

"You wish!"

Dashing forward, the cocky samurai screamed as he lunged on attack. Instantaneously, the other samurai parried the blow and ducked low, turning his sword back to his side. Then he brought it low in a half-circular motion. He thrust the sword upward, catching the cocky samurai off-guard.

Narrowly, he managed to get his sword in front of his face, which took a massive blow. A *Crack* reverberated through the air as his sword shattered into splinters just above the hilt. The end of the blade flew high into the air as the cocky samurai fell back, regaining his footing and landing a few feet away from his opponent.

The broken sword landed point down in the grass.

Looking at his broken sword, the cocky samurai yelled, "You bastard!"

With a smile, the calm samurai said, "Accept your defeat now, as a warrior."

Before he could finish, the cocky samurai dashed crazily toward him. Not expecting this, the calm one raised his sword to parry any attack. The cocky samurai used the few inches of blade left above his hilt to knock his opponent's sword back down. He grabbed the scruff of the calm one's shitogi with his left hand pinning his opponent's sword to the ground. He picked up his right foot and stepped on the sword, flexing it until it finally shattered near the hilt.

The calm samurai grabbed the crazy one's shitogi with his free hand, and both warriors poised their broken swords at each other. In the distance, a bell tolled at Edo Castle and there was a loud commotion outside. This didn't faze either warrior as they stared each other down. It was a stalemate.

An old, haggard woman shuffled up the hill. The warriors paid her no mind. It was the Dowager of Edo Castle. She stared at the Royal Guards, infuriated, and became even angrier seeing the two samurai, each pointing their broken weapons at each other's throat.

"Enough!"

Immediately, the Royal Guards jumped to their feet and began running back to Edo Castle.

"Tommy and Martin. How many times have I told you about playing with sticks?" she asked rhetorically. She grabbed both boys by the scruff of their shirts.

Coming to reality, both boys looked at her wide-eyed as they dropped their sticks.

"Recess is over. I suggest that both of you boys get back into the school before I bust a stick on you!" she scolded, letting them go.

They ran off in silence. They were warriors, but sometimes, the most strategic decision was choosing not to fight.

The Dowager watched the two samurai run back toward Edo Castle. She secretly smiled to herself.

"Those two," she shook her head. Secretly, she was proud that she could still cast fear into these children after so many years.

Tommy looked at Martin and said, "That was my favorite stick, you jerk!"

Martin replied calmly, "Are you going to cry?"

Tommy, who had dirty, messy clothing, looked back at him with a smile, "This isn't over."

"Not by a long shot," the calm samurai replied.

"Our duel will be decided next recess," the cocky samurai stated.

The contentious storm died, and the chartreuse sea was calm once again.

ABOUT THE AUTHOR

Match is a writer who has always enjoyed Horror. He has written several screenplays and enjoys writing stories and novels as well.

He graduated with an MBA with highest honors, and likes to use his education for his creative endeavors.

He is a proud husband father of four children. When he is not writing he spends time playing his guitar and singing in his band, Ricky London.

CONNECT WITH MATCH TENBRICK

You can find Match TenBrick and the Ricky London Band on social media at…

Facebook:

https://www.facebook.com/share/1FYBZM8Vd9/?mibextid=wwXIfr

Instagram:

- @Match.10
- @RickyLondonBand